MW00713501

THE SEARCH COMMITTEE

Also by Ralph McInerny:

FRIGOR MORTIS
LEAVE OF ABSENCE
THE NOONDAY DEVIL
CONNOLLY'S LIFE
ROMANESQUE
SPINNAKER
ROGERSON AT BAY
GATE OF HEAVEN
THE PRIEST
A NARROW TIME
JOLLY ROGERSON

The Andrew Broom Mystery Series

SAVINGS AND LOAM
BODY AND SOIL
CAUSE AND EFFECT

The Father Dowling Mystery Series

FOUR ON THE FLOOR
ABRACADAVER
THE BASKET CASE
REST IN PIECES
GETTING A WAY WITH MURDER
THE GRASS WIDOW
A LOSS OF PATIENTS
THICKER THAN WATER
SECOND VESPERS
LYING THREE
BISHOP AS PAWN
THE SEVENTH STATION
HER DEATH OF COLD

THE SEARCH COMMITTEE

Ralph McInerny

Atheneum New York 1991

Collier Macmillan Canada
Toronto

Maxwell Macmillan International
New York Oxford Singapore Sydney

This is a work of fiction. Names, characters, places, and incidents either are the product of the author's imagination or are used fictitiously. Any resemblance to events or persons, living or dead, is entirely coincidental.

Copyright © 1991 by Ralph McInerny

All rights reserved. No part of this book may be reproduced or transmitted in any form or by any means, electronic or mechanical, including photocopying, recording, or by any information storage and retrieval system, without permission in writing from the Publisher.

Atheneum
Macmillan Publishing Company
866 Third Avenue, New York, NY 10022

Collier Macmillan Canada, Inc.
1200 Eglinton Avenue East, Suite 200
Don Mills, Ontario M3C 3N1

Library of Congress Cataloging-in-Publication Data
McInerny, Ralph M.
The search committee / Ralph McInerny.
p. cm.
ISBN 0-689-12080-X
I. Title.
PS3563.A31166S38 1990
813'.54—dc20 90-45053 CIP

10 9 8 7 6 5 4 3 2 1

Printed in the United States of America

For Dave and Nancy

Contents

PROLOGUE

Hours of Gladness

Herbert Laplace, chancellor of the Fort Elbow campus of the University of Ohio, sat late in his office, a defiant tilt to his Barcalounger, a balloon glass held priestlike in both hands. A headset seemed to measure the balding expanse between his ears; tears streamed from his eyes.

The news had come just before his secretary left for the day, hours ago now. Rose gave him the message in the tone she used to tell him he was scheduled to speak a few words of greeting to some group convened on campus and he had received the news with corresponding everydayness. Someone identifying himself as Professor Felix Freeman had called from Arizona to say that Norah Vlach had died. "He said you would know," Rose said.

Watching his secretary leave the office on the invisible high wire over which she crossed the vicissitudes of life, Laplace realized he was ogling the woman, and at such a time. Strangely, the inappropriateness of his reaction lent additional poignancy to the moment. Norah dead. Dear, almost forgotten Norah Vlach was no more. He decided then and there to mourn her properly, she who had given him the comforts of her bed in exchange for tenure. Or so she had thought. It was only after they broke up that he told her of the unanimous recommendation of her department that she be promoted. Poor Norah had paid tribute for years to the wrong benefactor.

Once alone, Laplace poured out a brandy and solemnly toasted the memory of Norah. The gesture unexpectedly filled him with a sweet and irresistible wave of sadness. He sat at his desk, glass at his elbow, chronicling in his head the affair with Norah. Affair? That is how he thought of it now, although while it went on he taught himself to think of those Thursday afternoons as discrete events, each a pleasant little surprise rather than calculated routine. It had been important to his notion of himself that those silent and seldom satisfactory couplings in Norah's narrow bed seemed unexpected lapses or impetuous seductions. Actually, the arrangement had been so much like his marriage as to be redundant. But now it seemed important to remember as exactly as he could how many times he and Norah had done it.

Writing it down was like practicing a phrase in an odd language, an all but lost language now. No one had played Norah's role in his life for years—and as for Mrs. Laplacc, well, it was difficult to detect in the obese ruin of her body the concupiscible object of yore.

The next phase of his mourning found him doing undemanding exercises in a standing position in a corner of his office. He flung his arms wide and lifted on his toes in an imitation of wartime calisthenics, all the while making unkeepable resolutions. In the Age of Faith, the reminder of mortality had turned the thoughts of survivors to the condition of their soul; ascetic practices had suggested themselves. Laplace, an aging child of his time, promised himself he would return to jogging, taking it seriously this time, and to hell with the jeers of Matthew Rogerson. Why was he so vulnerable to the jealous taunts of that loser? Laplace brought his hands together, then flung his arms wide again, repeating the simple motion. Patty-cake, patty-cake. He firmly resolved that tomorrow he would once more follow the toes of his sneakers around the cork oval track in the field house, get his endurance gradually up to a mile, two miles, more. The vision of a slim self, hale and hearty, caused him to lower his heels, drop his hands and return satisfied to his desk. He stared at the sheet of paper and tried to evoke as vividly as he could what it had been like doing it with Norah.

He was on steady ground at last. He spent much time nowadays doing roughly this, reliving the triumphs of the past. And there were so many remembered triumphs. He was put in mind of a retort of Rogerson's when Laplace had asked, desperately seeking neutral ground, what the professor of Philosophy was reading.

"I don't read, Herb. I reread."

Just so, Herb sometimes felt that he did not so much live, as relive, the experiences that had been his before his prostate operation.

The third stage of mourning emerged from the second like a butterfly from a cocoon. Herb was drinking seriously now, and it was himself he mourned. It was only a matter of time then before he put on what he called his meditation tape and clamped the headset to his ears. It was a ninety-minute tape of his own editing. Music to feel self-pity by. Sounds to weep along with. The medley might not have moved another, but infallibly it reduced Chancellor Herbert Laplace to the sweet salt of self-indulgent tears.

There were long stretches of syrupy mood music arranged by Jackie Gleason, there were ten minutes of surf sounds, a

Tennysonian sea that broke on Laplace's ear in melancholy waves, and there was the scratchy voice of John McCormack, taped from the very records Laplace's mother had cherished. As an adolescent might resort to a favorite photo to stimulate his furtive fumbling, Laplace found the "Kerry Dances" unfailingly lachrymose.

> O the sound of the Kerry Dances,
> O the lilt of the piper's tune!
> Gone fore'er are those hours of gladness,
> Gone, alas, like our youth too soon.

He squeezed his eyes shut, hearing not only the voice of the dead tenor, but his mother's as well, singing along in a mingled keening and crooning. Her family had come from County Kerry, and though she had never seen the place herself, it was the country of her heart. And of her voice, too, when her Irish was up, and it not infrequently was because of her phlegmatic Franco-American husband. If only longevity had been in her blood. She at least would have regarded the chancellorship of what in unpronounceable acronym was called UOFE as eminence.

"UOFE," Rogerson would say, spelling it with relish. "Taking this place seriously is like believing in flying saucers."

As if the sonofabitch could have made the faculty anywhere else. No doubt Rogerson was jealous of Laplace's salary, if not his post. The chancellor's salary was pegged to that of the chancellor of the parent campus, the state's largess squandered by the legislature in a frenzy of provincial pride. Rogerson was one of the few who could remember what salaries had been like before postwar enthusiasm for higher education had lifted the Fort Elbow Normal School into the state university system. A rising tide lifts all boats.

Herbert Laplace, on the strength of a doctorate in education, moved from teaching elementary French to an assistant deanship. He became dean shortly after, at a time when real power went with the position, largely because of the ineptitudes of Wooley, the institution's first president in its new guise. Laplace then succeeded Wooley, the title of the post by then having been inflated along with everything else in academe. Now in his second five-year term, Chancellor Laplace could look out of his seventh-floor window in the Administration Building and survey a campus on which, as he liked to put it to businessmen and politicians, the life of the mind was pursued.

The phrase rang a little hollow when, unrecognized by students, he walked the paths of the campus. The student body was visible enough, but where was the student mind? Statistics from Student Health Services, reports of dormitory orgies and claims by female faculty of harassment by male scholars suggested that the student mind was somewhere below the belt. Still, no one could deny that the campus had a look of authenticity—Disney Productions had once considered shooting a film here. And in the mind of its chancellor, UOFE was Herbert Laplace and vice versa; if that seemed added reason for continuing to slop down brandy and cry his eyes out, so be it.

He was well on his way to wherever he was going when he became aware of the blurred figure of Matthew Rogerson standing by his desk. Laplace removed his headset and pushed a lever that returned his lounge chair to a more dignified level.

"How the hell did you get in here, Matt?"

"Are you giving yourself a balloon test?"

"Have a drink."

"Where's a glass?"

Herb gestured toward the wall. His liquor cabinet stood open; normally it was concealed behind a gaudily framed Botticelli print.

"Norah Vlach is dead."

They said the sentence simultaneously. Rogerson extended his hand and they locked little fingers. "Do you have any beer?"

"Beer drinkers never get this far. Besides, I thought you quit drinking."

"You have to in order to start again. Did Felix call you?"

"You too?"

"He always was a Cassandra."

"Yeah."

"The bearer of bad news."

"I heard you the first time."

Herb was not sure he wanted to share the mournful news with Rogerson. But a sip of brandy restored his spirits. "Sit down, Matt. The fact is, I've been sitting here remembering Norah."

"You ought to feel bad."

"I do."

"I mean guilty."

"Guilty! What the hell does that mean?"

Rogerson seemed a ghost from the past, sitting across from him, still wearing a goddam beard, no matter that he looked like an off-season Santa Claus. Who was Matthew Rogerson to sit in judgment on him? The goddam loser had been lucky to be kept on when UOFE moved into the big time. Herb imagined that he himself had saved Rogerson from hostile forces, and in a sense he had, stifling his urge to can Rogerson because of the flak he knew he would get from the remnant of the Old Bastards. Although Laplace had seniority over many of them, he had never been considered one of them, either by himself or by them. He had never felt fellowship and affinity with those relics of the school's past. Fellowship and affinity. Where had he stolen that?

Rogerson spoke quietly. "You ought to go home, Herb."

Laplace suddenly thought of Rogerson's wife, Marge. Six months after leaving Matt in search of a new life she was killed in a four-car crash on the Tamiami Trail.

Herb leaned forward, catching himself before he lost his balance. Someone with less tolerance for liquor than himself would be drunk after so much brandy. "How are you doing, Matt?"

"Doing?"

"Alone."

Rogerson's whiskered face twitched. "I did not know what loneliness was until I married. Chekhov."

"Don't, Matt. You'll go blind."

"Very funny." Rogerson rose. "Better sleep here, Herb."

Laplace looked at his watch but he could not make it out. He looked slyly at Rogerson.

"You had something going with Norah once, didn't you, Matt? Years ago."

"Something going." Rogerson repeated the words sadly and Laplace had the feeling he was receiving a bad grade.

"How would you put it?"

"I wouldn't, Herb. The next thing, you'll be telling me you had aspirations of your own."

"Aspirations!"

"Hopes. Plans. Designs."

"Goddam it, Matt, I know the word. The fact is, Norah and I . . ." He paused, but the brandy made anything possible now. "We loved one another, Matt. Who knows how these things begin? The truth is, I backed into it."

"Backed into what?"

"I don't want to talk about it."

"Do I hear singing?"

Laplace cocked his head as if to catch the strains of a celestial choir. But Rogerson stooped and picked up the headphones. He held them to one ear.

"That sounds like John McCormack."

"It is."

"The 'Kerry Dances'? I'm surprised it isn't 'Danny Boy.' "

"That comes later."

Rogerson frowned. "He's starting the 'Kerry Dances' again."

There were nearly twenty-five minutes of the "Kerry Dances"; the song played over and over. "I love that song."

Matt replaced the headset on the floor.

Laplace went recklessly on. "At this particular moment that song brings tears to my ears. 'Gone fore'er are those hours of gladness,/Gone, alas, like our youth too soon.' That says it all, doesn't it?"

"I would not willingly be one day younger than I am."

"You can't mean that."

"Hours of gladness." Rogerson shook his head.

"Have some brandy, Matt."

"Why the hell not? The fumes alone in here could make a man drunk."

It was better, much better, to have Rogerson there with a glass in his hand. Laplace now felt less self-conscious drinking from his own. By God, this was even better than the music, two old warriors from an earlier day, drinking a melancholy toast to a woman they had both shared a little pleasure with. A thought came to Herb, one of those errant wisps of wisdom alcohol will sometimes produce. "Things are better after they're over, Matt. When the only place they are is here." He tapped his head with two fingers. "Preserved."

"Pickled."

Herb was not to be baited. He was onto something deep and did not mean to let it go. However thick his tongue, his mind was clear.

"Look at all this, Matt." He made a sweeping gesture with his arm. "This place doesn't exist. It's less real than the office I had as dean and that building's been torn down. Remember the office you had in the basement of the library where you'd lock yourself in and get drunk?"

"It's still there. A juiceless cataloguer sits staring at a computer where my desk was."

"When did you go back?"

"When Felix was here . . ."

"When was Felix here?"

"I forget." Rogerson spoke evasively.

Had Felix Freeman, the quintessential Old Bastard, returned to the scene of his active years and not stopped by? Laplace felt cheated. "Why didn't he come see me?"

"He said let bygones be bygones."

"Good old Felix."

"Herb, he hates your guts."

"I know, I know. You get used to that."

"Three or four of us sat around and recalled what a shit you've been over the years."

"You should have invited me. Who all was there?"

Felix, Plummet-Finch, Schmidt. Herb poured more brandy for both of them, wanting to hear all about it. This was better than weeping over Norah Vlach. Of course the Old Bastards hated him. He would hate himself if he were a loser like them. It is the penalty of success to have jealous and resentful former friends. Of course none of them would ever admit how much they owed him, but hadn't they been spared when the dead wood was hacked out of the faculty?

Not that Laplace wanted thanks. The truth was he liked having them around as a visible reminder of how far he himself had come. Nor did he want to flirt with the legal trouble firing people could bring. The Old Bastards would have been delighted to take the administration to court and Wooley would have wanted to buy them off, laying out two or three years' salary in exchange for resignation. Why was it so pleasant to recall the Old Bastards as they had been?

"Say what you will, Matt, those were good times."

"Hours of gladness?"

"Yes! Oh, I know it was hard: low salaries, heavy teaching loads, marginal students, lousy offices and classrooms. But there was a spirit, Matt, a better spirit than we have now."

"How long do you plan to stay, Herb?"

"What do you mean?"

"When are you going to retire?"

"Retire! My God, I've got years to go before retirement."

"I thought we were the same age."

"That's what I'm saying."

"This is my final year, Herb. I've had it."

"Not me. I'm going until seventy."

"Why?"

"I have things to do yet, Matt. I haven't been shy about my ambitions for this campus."

"Forget the campus. I meant you."

He did not want to tell Rogerson that this was all he was. If he had been a praying man, he would pray to die in office, with his loafers on. But not yet. Make it as close to the mandatory retirement age as possible. He had the sense he should promise God something in return, but he couldn't think what it might be.

"You plan to go live in the desert with Felix, Matt?"

"Oh, no. I'll stay in Fort Elbow."

"Marge is buried here, isn't she?" Herb had memories of the funeral, between Thanksgiving and Christmas, colder than a gravedigger's ankle, everyone pretending Marge had been vacationing in Florida and had not filed for divorce. Did Matt plan to lie beside her under the snow?

"I heard you were retiring," Rogerson said.

"Bullshit."

"That's what they're saying at the Faculty Club."

"Who started it, you?"

"I was the one who denied it, Herb. Once you had the soul of a dean. Now you have the soul of a chancellor. Chancellor of a nothing campus in the state system. This is your destiny. You belong here."

"No one can say I haven't done a good job."

"Can and do, Herb, and I am of their number." Rogerson finished his brandy and held out his glass. "I came over here to tell you off. You weren't at home, I haven't heard that you have another floozy, and the lights were on here. Elementary. I wanted to make sure you weren't pretending to mourn Norah Vlach. You weren't fit to kiss her foot."

Herb nodded. "You were jealous of her too, weren't you?"

"Too?"

"Also."

Rogerson was on his feet again. He couldn't be drunk. He had had only a few ounces of brandy.

"Herb, I could tell you what Norah thought of you but that would be to break a confidence. I could tell you about Norah and me, but I won't. All I have to say is this. Don't mourn for her, Herb. Feel sorry for yourself, imagine some past when you weren't a sonofabitch, if you can, get drunk and cry into your booze, but goddam it, leave Norah out of it. Is that fireplace real?"

"It's a helluva lot realer than you are, Rogerson."

Rogerson threw his glass into the fireplace. It broke with a pop on the electric log. Matt tugged at the door twice before he got it open, enough time for Laplace to get the last word.

"I was going to ask you to retire early, Rogerson. Force it if I had to."

The music was not the same when he was alone again. The brandy had lost its strength, running down his throat like water and with as little further effect. He turned off the tape, put the brandy back behind the Botticelli and, closing one eye, made out the time. The idea was like a cloud formation on his mind's horizon. He nodded in assent.

He drove in his Mercedes to Morton, twenty miles southwest of Fort Elbow where, on the outskirts, there was a massage parlor. More than one kind of turnover characterized the place: the girls seemed always different. Once he had been attended by a redhead who claimed to be a student at UOFE and he knew a moment of panic. But who could be more anonymous to students than a naked chancellor? The place was sleazy, the walls of the rooms covered with carpeting as if the girls might defy gravity and walk up to the ceiling. Lying on an altarlike bed, Laplace nearly swooned as the brandy made itself felt. He wondered if his legs could carry him back to the car. It was clear that his body was in no condition for this. The girl stood nurselike beside him, her voice mingling sadness and contempt as they agreed there was nothing doing. If he had been sober he might have been ashamed. The girl helped him dress after he danced across the room on one leg trying to pull on his trousers. He tipped her lavishly and she escorted him out to his car.

"You shouldn't drive."

"I'll take a little nap."

She left him. He opened the roof and tipped back his head. If you drink don't drive. He couldn't agree more. He had made a TV spot for MADD aimed particularly at students. A patrol car went slowly past the lot. Laplace decided he would go home and get some sobering sleep there. It would not do to have the chancellor of UOFE caught napping in the parking lot of a massage parlor in Morton.

Back on the highway, headed for Fort Elbow, he gave the Mercedes the gas, eager now to be home and in his own bed. He heard the siren first, then saw the flashing lights in his rearview mirror. He was drunk and driving. Not only that, he was speeding. He tromped down on the gas. There was no patrol car that could match the Mercedes in power.

He was right. The distance between him and the flashing lights increased and he could no longer hear the siren. He had done it. Thank God! He was promising never again to get behind the wheel after so much as a bottle of beer when he saw flashing lights ahead.

Had they passed him? Impossible. He slowed, flicking off his headlights as he did, looking for his chance. Then he found it, a link between the two divisions of the road. He swung left before his speed was sufficiently reduced and the gravelly shoulder made the car spin. Herb gripped the wheel but there was nothing he could do. The Mercedes rolled over once and then halfway again, ending up on its roof with the suspended chancellor—he had not forgotten to buckle up—breathing heavily, full of fear, but uninjured. The sound of the sirens and the sight of the flashing lights were almost welcome now.

PART ONE

The Stag at Eve

Chapter One

1

Valerie Kraft, her ankle-length robe belted low on her hips, a towel wrapped around her just-shampooed iron-gray hair, came from the shower to turn on the morning news. Through four commercials, she rubbed her hair damp if not dry. The blower would do the rest. And without delay, she decided, when the idiot whose hair looked like Harpo Marx's began to read the sports results. His image wavered as Valerie pointed her hair dryer at her head and flicked the switch.

She must try to acquire an interest in sports. Nothing human should be alien to her. This somewhat quaint Humanist creed was the only one she had, and she was more of a backslider than a true believer. Think of what a list all things human would make. Besides, most of them were engaged in by men, not human beings.

She imagined the ceiling sliding back and an eye in the sky looking in at her. A chunky figure in a maroon robe, the line of her jaw growing indistinct, regretting the decision to stop dyeing her hair, living alone and hating it. Thoughts of Carlotta needled her and she directed the dryer around the room as if it were a ray gun. Forget that bitch. Forget the minuses in her life. The pluses more than outbalanced them.

Vice-provost—and dear God the tired jokes that prefix provoked—the highest-ranked woman in the hierarchy of UOFE, and her ambitions did not stop at this God forsaken campus. Her degree was from the University of Chicago, the Committee on Social Thought, her dissertation a must on any bibliography dealing with FDR's Brain Trust. She had taught at Chicago, U Conn and Northern Illinois before the notice of the vice-provost search at the Fort Elbow campus caught her eye. She sent in her resumé. She was interviewed, trying to mask the contempt she felt for the place and for the committee—except for Carlotta, of course. She made the short list and would have been surprised if she had not been offered the job. Dickering over salary with the ridiculous Laplace made it clear that she would have no trouble handling him. The provost? All old Handel wanted was to be left alone. He had a microfilm reader in his office and turned blinking guiltily from it whenever she went in to see him. He was a medievalist, by definition mad, but endearing in the way he turned everything over to Valerie.

"You're the answer to a prayer, my dear." She might have taken umbrage at the sexist implications, the condescension—would he be describing her as a jewel next?—but she contented herself with warning him about the separation of church and state. He had frowned in incomprehension and, inexperienced with Handel's obtuseness, she tried to explain. She never made that mistake again. For her sins—another of Handel's expressions—she tried to read one of the offprints he gave her, an unintelligible discussion of Rhineland mysticism.

"I thought you would be interested in Hildegaard of Bingen."

"Thank you."

"Because she was a woman," he added with a little giggle.

What had the old fart meant by that? Nothing, apparently; nonetheless Valerie turned on the feminine charm for a day or two, without visible effect on Handel. But it had flushed Carlotta out of the closet.

The image on the television screen snapped her out of it. Herb Laplace? She turned off the dryer but caught only the end of a sentence before the still photo gave way to a local team of announcers. Where did they find these people? More important, what item of news had involved Herb Laplace?

Valerie hurried to the kitchen and flicked on the radio. For an annoying ten minutes she turned from one station to another, but even when she did find a news broadcast, there was no mention of Laplace. Finally, WFEO rewarded her with a wrap-up. She could not stifle a whoop when she heard that Dr. Herbert Laplace, chancellor of the University of Ohio at Fort Elbow, had been arrested early that morning for driving under the influence and attempting to evade arrest. There had been an accident but the educator had been uninjured.

This was too funny to be true!

Valerie's hand went to the phone but stopped. Whom could she call?

Careful, careful, she told herself. She must not overlook the significance for herself of this public disgrace. This meant the end of the chancellor. He could never overcome the negative effects of such an episode. Laplace would be forced to resign, and what then?

Acting chancellor. Valerie Kraft, acting chancellor. The words formed slowly in her mind. Was that possible? A hurried mental shuffling of the alternatives made it seem not only possible but inevitable. Handel would refuse even if he were asked, which seemed unlikely. Morgan, the dean? He was too new in that job. Harrigan, the comptroller? He was a number cruncher, and he knew it. The one figure Valerie had trouble dismissing out of hand was Kessel, the assistant to the chancellor.

Kessel was such a beautiful young man that Valerie had wondered about Laplace, but there was nothing like that involved. The chancellor's lusts were severely heterosexual and he seemed to think he had seignorial rights to every woman on the faculty and staff. Valerie herself had had to withstand a halfhearted approach from Laplace. She might have acquiesced even in that if she had thought it would help her career, but Laplace's gesture at seduction had carried no implication of the fury of the scorned. Kessel. Blond wavy hair, built like a brick chateau, a classicist, of all things, an expert in the transmission of the poems of Catullus, Kessel had left the classroom without regret and Valerie doubted he ever intended to return. Kessel was a threat but he was only thirty-one. Valerie felt she had him beaten in every department but one. Kessel was a man.

When Valerie finally snatched the phone from the hook and dialed Carlotta it was anything but a calculated act. She had to talk to someone and who better than Carlotta?

Even the ringing in her ears seemed familiar, which was fanciful. But was it fanciful to imagine that Laplace's plight might bring them back together again, Carlotta and herself? What is more unifying than the misfortune of a common enemy?

2

Handel began the day with Bach, not with the garbled accounts of the doings of little men that was called news. Nothing in Rhenish mysticism was too trivial to hold his interest, but the most shattering events of his own time remained largely unknown to the provost. He forced himself to read the *Week in Review* in the Sunday *Times*, but most of it was unintelligible to him. How could the disasters of the day compete with the correspondence between Bernard of Clairvaux and Hildegaard of Bingen? This morning, the ominous news about Laplace was conveyed to the provost by Mrs. Handel.

Laura listened to the television wearing an enormous pair of earphones—to spare him, but also in order to hear. They had spent eight hundred dollars for the hearing aid that she refused to wear, not out of vanity—her thick hair more than concealed the device—but out of annoyance that it did not restore the acute hearing of her girlhood.

"Laplace has been arrested," she shouted through the strains of a concerto.

Handel nodded. It was best not to encourage these attempts on Laura's part to mediate between him and the world.

"He tried to get away but they ran him down. His car rolled over one and a half times."

"What is half a roll?" And so he had been undone by this pedantry. He could no longer ignore Laura.

"The car came to a stop on its roof."

"Was he killed?"

"They wouldn't have arrested him if he were dead."

Good point. And then the enormity of what she had said broke through the baroque measures of Bach and he lifted the arm from the record.

"Laplace has actually been arrested?"

She pointed to the television where the smiling face of Herbert Laplace was just fading away.

Handel had to wait through twenty minutes of electronic

torture before the story was told again. In a phrase from his youth, he offered it up. Finally, the local news rolled around again and Herbert Laplace was indeed the lead story.

Driving while drunk. Laura had gotten that right after all. Nor had she overdramatized the way in which Laplace had been taken into custody. Imagine trying to outrace the police! But then, when one was drunk one would attempt irrational things. A teetotaler himself, Handel had seen at parties what drink did to otherwise rational beings. And so quickly.

"I suppose they'll fire him," Laura said. She spoke these words as if unaware they were the moral equivalent of an earthquake.

"Fire a chancellor?"

However unthinkable the thought, Handel could not dismiss it from his mind once it had gained entry with Laura's insouciant remark. The depths to which Laplace had apparently fallen and the probable consequences of his indiscretion made Handel physically weak. It seemed likely that Laplace would resign before he could be fired, thereby retaining a shred of dignity. It went without saying that his public humiliation would rob him of the necessary authority to direct the affairs of the Fort Elbow campus.

Handel did not hold this campus of the state system in the contempt common among the faculty. That there were more distinguished universities, that higher salaries might be available elsewhere, that one might easily have colleagues more distinguished than those here—these were truths which did not achieve a level of importance in Handel's mind. The fact was that he was already acquainted with every scholar with interests similar to his own and each of them lived a life of isolation from the rest. Nor did Handel feel any need for daily intercourse with any of his fellow specialists. Better to correspond with them, chitchat at the annual meeting of the Medieval Academy and pursue alone the spoor of his research. Cohorts, he had come to believe, are of limited help in the quest of truth.

"Who will take his place?" Laura asked.

"The place of Laplace." But he took no pleasure in the redundancy. It was upsetting enough that the chancellor must step down in disgrace, but Laura in her annoying way pointed to something more upsetting still.

"I don't want to think about it."

"You are the obvious choice."

"Don't say that! You are being cruel. I will not be asked and if I were I would not accept."

She smiled. "You said the same thing about becoming provost."

She was right. So he had. And what unshirted hell being provost had been until Laplace pointed out the obvious solution.

"Handel, you are the only administrator who does not have an assistant to do your job. Hire an associate provost."

"Can I do that?"

"Of course. Just write it into your next budget."

Was it that simple? It was. The fact that he had not known so obvious a thing should have strengthened his case that he be allowed to resign but Laplace would not hear of it.

"You've remained a scholar, Handel. That is important. It gives us all a little class. They eat it up in Columbus when I tell them of my publishing provost. So get someone to take care of your paperwork and you stick to that machine." He meant the microfilm reader. Then Laplace stated what he clearly regarded as a stronger reason.

"It's a relief to work with someone without ambition, Handel. You're not after my job."

"Your job!" Handel shook his head in horror. Laplace smiled.

"And I believe you. You may be the only one not after my job or anything else that turns up in the *Chronicle*."

"The chronicle?"

"The *Chronicle of Higher Education*. Even Kessel pores over the damned thing. Why can't he read the *Wall Street Journal* like Harrigan?"

Handel advertised for a vice-provost, aided by Kessel. As soon as he talked with Valerie Kraft, he saw the wisdom of Laplace's suggestion. This woman, trying unsuccessfully to be deferential, obviously yearned to have the job of doing Handel's work for him. He hired her, and ever since, life had been idyllic. Not that she was unique. He would have been satisfied with any of the candidates.

"We need a broad," Laplace said, and that was that.

Now, to Laura, in self-defense but realizing as he said it how much he meant it, he chirped, "I have my candidate."

"Who?"

"Valerie Kraft."

3

"Who was it?" Carlotta asked with forced nonchalance when Kessel eased the phone back onto its cradle.

"I think it was Valerie."

Several scenarios unrolled rapidly behind Carlotta's eyes, but she retained control of herself.

"And you hung up on her?"

"I was thinking of your good name."

"Never answer a lady's phone before nine in the morning."

"Is that what they taught you at Annapolis?"

Carlotta had come through four years of the Academy as a midshipperson, put in two years on active duty, enough to surmise that she would never go to sea because she was too valuable to the fleet in Washington, requested leave to attend graduate school and actually wangled Navy financing for her doctorate.

The phone began to ring again. Carlotta snatched it up. The infuriated voice of Valerie Kraft hissed in her ear.

"Don't you ever hang up on me again!"

"Was that you just now? Actually it was Peter Kessel who hung up the phone."

"Peter Kessel!" There was a brief pause.

"I suppose he just had to talk to somebody," Valerie said in altered tones. Carlotta had been waiting for Valerie to slam down the phone this time. "I feel the same way."

"Well . . ." Carlotta said, crossing her eyes in confusion.

"Let me talk to Peter."

"You have to talk to someone," Carlotta agreed, handing the phone to Peter, who moved out of range of it. "She wants to talk to you."

Peter reluctantly took the phone and Carlotta went off to scramble eggs. She decided that Peter's answering the phone had indeed been a good thing in the circumstances. How better to convince Val that she had turned over a new page, as the congressman said. A man answering an early-morning call was a far more convincing argument than any she might have devised. Such consoling thoughts distracted her from what Peter was saying, and it came as a mild surprise to find that he had hung up the phone and come into the kitchen.

"What's wrong?"

"Did you catch the drift of that conversation?"

"I'm scrambling eggs."

"Where's a radio?"

"In the bedroom."

"I have to phone Huile."

It didn't seem all that important to Carlotta when she finally got the picture. So what if Laplace had had a little too much to drink? Since when was that a crime?

"It becomes one when you get behind the wheel of a car and endanger the lives of others. And your own." Peter was imitating Laplace. "His very words. Did you see the TV spot he did on drunk driving?"

"I don't have a TV."

For the first time he looked at her as if he saw more than a body. Did he imagine an intransigent intellectual who refused to let a river of rot into her apartment? Was that the meaning of "down the tube?" The fact is she had never acquired the habit of watching television. If she bought one, she would want it to be portable and ignorable, like a radio. Who ever actually listens to radio?

Peter Kessel, as it happened; he was huddled over her little Sony expectantly. He nodded through the account of Laplace's arrest. He picked up the phone and dialed again the number that had not responded the first time. Success.

"Huile? Peter Kessel. What are we going to do?"

The expression on his face suggested that he was not impressed by Huile's proposed agenda. He shook his head as he listened.

"Forget it, Ollie. There is no way we can play this down. Start working on a resignation statement. Yes, resignation. As in Duke of Windsor and Richard Nixon. Short and sweet.

No bullshit. He was caught with his pants down and that's that. Not even you could make this look good."

But he had to listen to more of Huile. This time he laughed.

"If I ever get in trouble, remind me to call you. Look. I'll phone Mayhew. We'll meet at my office in half an hour."

"What was his plan?" Carlotta asked when he had hung up.

Kessel laughed again. "He thought we might claim the whole thing was staged by Laplace and the cops to dramatize the dangers of driving drunk. Just another public service from the chancellor."

"It might work."

"Maybe. If only Laplace had called Huile last night."

"Did he call anyone else?"

"Maybe me."

"Oh."

"I've got to run." His expression became serious as he gripped her upper arms and looked deeply into her eyes. She wasn't sure of the significance of this but she looked deeply back into his.

When he was gone she turned off the radio and ate her breakfast. And his. Far more scrambled eggs than she wanted, but she could not bear to throw out good food. But all that cholesterol! She would atone by missing lunch.

Valerie did not answer when Carlotta called her back. The fog was lifting from her mind and she began to see why Peter and Val and apparently others were so excited by the morning news. Maybe this wasn't just a little pip of scandal that would thrive for a day or two and then die away. What would happen if Laplace actually did resign?

Carlotta had no idea of the procedure for naming a successor. The appointment was made by the governor, wasn't it, or was it the legislature? Or both? In any case there would be at least a pro forma consultation with the faculty. Would the next chancellor, like Laplace himself, be chosen from the ranks of the faculty? Carlotta did not know how this sort of thing worked.

Valerie Kraft as chancellor? The thought did not seem absurd to her. That Valerie herself might think it possible would explain the phone call and the remark that she had to talk with someone about the disgrace of the chancellor. If she and Peter had concluded that Laplace would be forced to resign, Valerie's thoughts must have run on to his successor. And Valerie was more than convinced of her ability to do any job a man could do and probably do it better.

As Valerie saw it, sexism makes the world go around. Nothing happened that did not emerge from the conspiracy of the male gender. Even Valerie's dubious sexual orientation seemed ideological, a conclusion rather than a passionate premise.

Not that she wasn't sweet. Carlotta dialed again and got an answer.

"Dr. Kraft, please."

"The vice-provost is not in the office," Basil, her secretary, said prissily. "I can take a message."

"Tell her Carlotta called."

"Carlotta! I didn't recognize your voice. Forgive me. Val is all tied up because of the big scandal. You heard about Laplace?"

"Val told me. Will he resign?"

"If he isn't fired, darling. If he isn't fired."

4

Acting as university counsel had cured Gil Mayhew of a dream that plagues the successful lawyer, of serving a stint on a law faculty. Once this had seemed to promise relief from the pressure and pettiness of the firm in which he had twenty partners, forty associates and God knows how many paralegals and others. Another dream, an undemanding judgeship in which he could live out his days writing opinions that would leave members of the bar, junior and senior, awestruck, was too close to his daily routine to remain realistic. But, oh, a classroom far from the litigious ways of men in which he could lecture to youth still inexperienced in the world beyond. That dream had been a casualty of contact with the actual academic world. Serving as university counsel was like returning to the playground.

Herb Laplace had actually wept when Mayhew went down to post bail for him.

"Gil, please get me out of here."

"You can come with me now."

"I was afraid that bastard Rogerson forgot to call you."

"He called."

"When?"

"Last night."

Herb looked at him with red-rimmed, tear-filled eyes. "And you let me spend the night here?"

"Nothing could be done until this morning, Herb. Even so, I had to roust out Harrison this morning and he was all for denying bail."

"The sonofabitch."

"One of your fellow crusaders against the menace of drink."

Judge Harrison, white-haired, everyone's grandfather, his

iron and irony not captured by the camera, had pleaded with drinkers to leave their cars alone. "Because, my friends, if you drive under the influence and are brought before me, I will show you no mercy. None." How sweet he looked when he said it, as if it would hurt him more than the poor sot who stood before his bench. Harrison was AA and should have disqualified himself from trying DUI's. The man was a zealot.

"Will that count in my favor?" Herb asked.

"A night in this place has muddled your mind. It will count against you."

"What do you plan to do?"

"Escort you out of here. You don't need any more publicity."

"More?"

"You're a media sensation. You've made the morning news, every hour on the hour."

"What are they saying?" Herb was recovering his self-respect now that they had emerged from the antiseptic reek of the drunk tank, passed the guard and come to a bank of elevators.

"Don't you remember what happened?"

"That's a cheap shot, Gil."

"They're saying you tried to outrace the policeman who noticed your erratic driving, that you turned out your lights and spun out and rolled your car and are lucky to be alive. You insisted on taking the balloon test and may have set a new indoor record. You're in trouble."

"That's why I have a lawyer."

"Correction. I am the university's lawyer." The distinction made Herb squirm as it was meant to.

Mayhew asked himself what image he would have had of a university chancellor, even of so modest a campus as the Fort Elbow one, if he had not come to know Herb Laplace.

But analogous disillusion had set in when he first came to know senior partners, judges, senators, the governor. No man is a hero to his lawyer. Hero? Mayhew would have settled for a modicum of maturity. Well, Laplace's days as chancellor were over.

"Where are we going?" Herb asked as they rose in the elevator.

"To the thirteenth floor. Traffic Court. Harrison's chambers. He has agreed to chew you out in private. Then we meet with Kessel and Huile."

"Good."

Herb was not referring to Harrison when he said that.

Traffic Court was reminiscent of railway waiting rooms of yore, not looking like a place where justice was meted out, but Harrison's chambers resembled a Hollywood set. Harrison sat like Andy Hardy's father behind a huge desk at the far end of the room. There was nothing on the desk before him but his thin hands and he peered nearsightedly at his approaching visitors.

"This is not to be construed as preferential treatment," Harrison began. "But of course it is. We can expect the media to raise a howl." He moved his hands, then put them back where they had been. "That is why I agreed to Mr. Mayhew's request. I want all the howling I can get, Chancellor Laplace. You are a disgrace to the university. I assume that you intend to resign."

"Resign!" Laplace spluttered, and Mayhew laid a hand on his arm.

"Your Honor, Dr. Laplace is here to plead Not Guilty to the charge of driving under the influence and attempting to evade arrest. . . ."

"Did you say Not Guilty?"

". . . and to ask for a jury trial."

"Good! I set bail at fifty thousand dollars."

"Would Your Honor consider reducing that to twenty-five thousand? Dr. Laplace is unlikely to leave the jurisdiction of the court."

"Twenty-five it is. We will schedule the trial for next week. I will save what I have to say until the trial."

Until the conviction is what he meant.

"I don't have twenty-five thousand dollars," Laplace squeaked as they left Harrison's chambers.

"You only need twenty-five hundred. Use a credit card."

5

Oliver Huile wore a baggy corduroy coat whose pockets bulged with the weirdest assortment of paraphernalia, yet whatever Ollie sought in them was never there. At the moment, he had just proved to himself and Kessel that he had not brought with him the statement that Herb Laplace would have to be persuaded to issue.

The phone rang and Enid mouthed the message. "The state senator."

Kessel went alone into his inner office to take the call. The senator was Rod Bellini, who considered, not without reason, that the appointive posts on the Fort Elbow campus were his gift. Thanks to him, Kessel had been picked from a sea of candidates for assistant to the chancellor. One might have thought the chancellor would choose his own assistant, and so, in a sense, he had; but Peter Kessel had had a hunch that the swarthy man seated in a corner of the office, arms folded, silently following the interview, was more important than he looked. He had not been introduced to the candidate but the man's manner suggested he was monitoring Laplace as well as Kessel. When the interview was over, Kessel had crossed the room and put out his hand. The man looked up at him over those folded arms and there was a terrible moment when Kessel thought he was going to be snubbed. But then a fat and furry hand came forth to shake his own.

"This is State Senator Bellini," Laplace then said, a little breathlessly.

"I thought I recognized you, sir," Kessel lied.

He left the room in the certainty that he had the job.

The significance of the moment came home to him now when he realized that he was standing as he took the call.

"How bad is it, Peter?"

"Obviously you will have heard. Why ask?"

"It could blow over in days."

"Not on campus. Students are merciless and unimaginative and Herb has always been the favorite butt of the student paper."

"What have you advised him to do?"

"We're scheduled to meet in half an hour. Who has the power to fire him?"

"The newspapers."

"I'm serious, Senator."

"So am I. Technically, Horkimer is the cabinet officer with responsibility for the university system. But the weakest television channel has more power than he does. Think of it, Kessel. A man to whom the people of this state have entrusted their children stands revealed as a public drunk, which makes him a hypocrite as well, after that TV spot. What the hell was he doing in Morton anyway?"

"Probably visiting a massage parlor."

There was an intake of breath at the other end of the line. Senator Bellini was shocked. "Tell him to resign."

"I couldn't agree more."

"What about his successor?"

Kessel's mouth was suddenly dry. "How do you mean, Senator?"

"Do you have the confidence of your colleagues?"

"That's not for me to say."

"Cut the bullshit."

"Yes, I do."

"Then make your move. You're my candidate, Kessel."

"Thank you, Senator. Would you like Laplace to call you?"

"What for?"

Bellini hung up. Kessel sat and for a full minute savored this turn of events. Chancellor Kessel? Why not? He buzzed Enid and told her to send Huile in. When the PR man sidled in, scratching his head, peering over the top of his cloudy glasses, Kessel suddenly felt like a chancellor. He made an impatient gesture when Huile apologized for losing the statement.

"What did it say, Ollie?"

Huile earned his living with his pen but was virtually tongue-tied in conversation. The pen is mightier for the surd.

"I had him thanking people for their help and support."

Kessel shook his head. "No. It has to be three or four declarative sentences. Nothing abject. Let him go out with dignity. Remember when Henry Ford was picked up on the same charge? Never apologize, never explain."

"He was quoting," Huile said.

"So am I. That's our guide. You can mention the pressures

of the job, the loneliness at the top, that sort of thing." He stopped. Ollie was grimacing.

"I got the idea."

"You want to use Enid's typewriter, go ahead."

Ollie had written a sentence and a half when Laplace and Mayhew arrived. Herb looked like hell. He hadn't shaved, his eyes were bloodshot and he kept looking over people's heads and making an odd groaning sound.

"Ollie is preparing a statement for you, Herb."

"Yeah."

"Short and sweet."

"Forget the statements," Herb snarled, suddenly his old self. He glared at Ollie. "Did I ask you to write a statement?"

Ollie shrugged, pulled the paper from the typewriter and put his sentence and a half in his pocket.

Mayhew intervened. "Let me see what you wrote."

Ollie actually had trouble finding the damned thing. Mayhew smoothed it out and took it to the window to get the light of day on it. They all awaited his reaction. He brought it back to the desk, leaned over and added several lines, then gave the sheet to Herb.

Herb's lower lip trembled as he read the message. He kept his eyes fixed on the paper long after he had read it.

"Try it out loud," Mayhew said.

"I am not going to resign!"

"Herb, you haven't any choice."

"What the hell is this, Russia? If I don't want to resign, I won't resign. What have I done, after all?"

"Disgraced the university," Mayhew said calmly.

"Senator Bellini called," Kessel said. "He advises you to resign."

"Bellini said that?" Herb's mouth remained open. If

Bellini was against him, who would be for him? He looked again at the piece of paper. He cleared his throat. Only on the third try did he manage to read it aloud.

"Today I am resigning as chancellor of the Fort Elbow campus, having held office for some seven years. I will not cite the accomplishments of those years, nor the heavy toll they have taken on me personally. There is a season for all things. My season has ended. God bless you."

" 'God bless you'?" Kessel queried.

"How about 'Have a nice day'?" Ollie said unblinkingly.

"It's a nice touch," Mayhew said. "I mean 'God bless you.' Corny but disarming. It suggests a penitent man yet makes no admissions."

"It has dignity," Kessel said, and Laplace's shoulders straightened.

"Class," Huile agreed.

A serious but satisfied expression brought tautness to Herb's unshaven jaw. The room was silent for half a minute.

"Release it, Ollie," Herb said, and the die was cast.

Kessel came around his desk and put an arm around the now as-good-as former chancellor. "Get cleaned up and we'll videotape it in the campus studio for immediate release."

"No pretrial interviews," Mayhew reminded Laplace.

Visibly now Laplace assumed his role in the drama, apparently convinced he was in the hands of experts and friends.

"We will want Mrs. Laplace at your side," Kessel said.

"No! Leave her out of this."

"She's in it, Herb. She's a must. The sustaining spouse. You've seen it a hundred times."

Herb's eyes narrowed in thought. "You're right. She's a sport. She'll be good."

Well, good was a little strong. They looked like a pair of

mourners in the studio lights. Clean-shaven, Herb looked chalky and gaunt, as if he had been on a week-long toot.

Matt Rogerson sat next to Ollie in the darkness enveloping the brightly lit set. More moral support? It was hard to say.

"Ollie," Rogerson said in a stage whisper. "I want a copy of this for my VCR. This is a day I've dreamed of."

Rogerson as vulture? Not that either. When it was over, when Mayhew nodded toward the exit and Kessel was following the lawyer out, he turned and looked back at the dimmed stage where Rogerson had taken Mrs. Laplace into his arms and held her as she cried helplessly.

6

"It's over now, Lillie," Rogerson crooned, and it was like consoling a widow. The thought brought an unbidden memory of Marge and tears started up in his own eyes. He released Lillie and she turned to Herb. It was the first crack she had had at him since the arrest.

"What in the name of God were you up to last night?"

"Before I spun out? Eighty. Maybe eighty-five. I had it right down on the floor." But he didn't move too fast for Lillie. "Ouch!"

She had dug her nails into his hand. "Don't talk smart to me now, not after this. Do you realize what you've done?"

Herb tried to smile at Rogerson but it was a grotesque failure. Rogerson might be safely widowed, but Herb should have realized he remembered what marriage is like.

"Yesterday I got word that Norah Vlach is dead," Herb said to Lillie.

"Norah Vlach?"

"She worked here for years. In my office for a while."

"The mousy woman with the big boobs?"

"You could write copy for Ollie," Herb growled, already regretting his lapse into sincerity.

Lillie turned to Rogerson while retaining a grip on her husband's hand. "Norah Vlach. This one shacked up with her, did you know that, Matt?"

"We all did, Lillie."

"What?"

"Now it can be told," Rogerson continued. "This campus is worse than you imagine. Everybody doing it with everybody else all the time. Isn't that what you imagine? With Herb on top of the heap?"

"Be serious."

"You be serious, Lillie. This dumdum of a husband of yours could use a little support. Not that he deserves it. What do you say?"

"What do I say?" She moved so close to Rogerson he could feel her belly against his. She had tugged Herb along when she moved. They might have been one of the trios she imagined Herb in when he didn't come home. "I say I'm glad. Mr. Chancellor here has been too big for his britches for years. Joke all you want but I know what he's been up to. I know why he drove all the way to Morton blind drunk. Heartbroken for Norah and mourning her the only way he knows."

Rogerson pretended to be distracted by something behind her. "Is that camera still running?"

Lillie leaped back, turned toward the nonexistent camera, then began to beat furiously on Rogerson's chest.

"Better try mouth-to-mouth, Lillie. That method never works with me."

"You're two of a kind! You always were. I hate you both."

And Lillie went streaking from the studio, her going followed by half a dozen goggle-eyed student technicians. Rogerson turned to Laplace, nodding judiciously.

"Personally, I think she's perfect for the part. I say no more auditions. Agreed?"

"Yeah," Herb said. "Let's get the hell out of here."

They went to Herb's office, entering like interlopers. Rose looked up, her mouth fishlike in surprise. "No calls," Herb said as he went by her desk. In the inner office, Herb stood in the middle of the oversized room, looking around in bewildered fashion. His eyes met Rogerson's.

"Just last night, Matt. And now it's over."

"Get out the brandy."

"That's not funny."

"I mean it."

Herb cocked his head, then rolled out his lower lip. "A hair of the dog. You're right."

"Put on 'Danny Boy.' "

"Not until after we've heard the 'Kerry Dances.' "

They sang along, why the hell not? Rose looked in, horrified, and Rogerson waved.

"No visitors."

"Are you two crazy?"

"When you have a minute, come in and toast the former chancellor."

She looked at Herb. "Is it true?"

"I have laid down the burden of office, yes."

"Jesus. I'll be back."

She came back when "Danny Boy" was on and did not stay long, perhaps put off by the tears in the eyes of two grown men. Neither was sorry to see her go. The way she drank off the brandy suggested a thirsty woman.

The phone rang several times after she left. Did Dr. Laplace wish to speak to the press? Would Dr. Laplace take

Mr. Mayhew's call? Senator Bellini's office had left a number where the senator could be reached. Herb ignored them all.

"Reduced to the ranks," Rogerson mused.

"Can you see me in a classroom again, Matt?"

"On which side of the desk?"

Later Herb said, "The whole thing would have blown over, Matt. Maybe I should have stalled."

"I think the term of art is stonewalled."

"They set me up for it, Matt. They had the statement prepared. I wasn't ready; I was pushed."

"They did you a favor."

Herb's eyes grew large as John McCormack breathed an Ave.

"What hurt, Matt, was that they were enjoying it. I felt that."

"You may be right."

"I know I'm right." Herb looked with moist eyes at Rogerson. "Matt, you're the only friend I have."

"You poor sonofabitch."

Chapter Two

1

To the interpretation of the *Faculty Manual,* particularly those paragraphs dealing with the senate, Abe Herman, despite his weakness for the hermeneutic excesses of colleagues in the English Department, brought a rabbinic meticulousness. He approached each sentence, each clause, and each word in them, as the expression of a deliberate act of choice entailing hundreds of exclusions.

"There is no provision," he repeated to Valerie Kraft, "for the appointment of a chancellor search committee by the steering committee of the Faculty Senate."

"How can such a committee be constituted?"

"A motion could be made from the floor."

"But the steering committee of which you and I are members prepares motions in advance of meetings."

Herman conceded the point with a reluctant dip of his bald head.

"Abe, if we can authorize a motion, we can also name the committee. This is an emergency."

"If it were, it would be provided for by the *Faculty Manual*."

"The *Faculty Manual* was not given by God to Moses on Mount Sinai."

"Is that a racial slur?"

"Oh, come on."

"What did you mean by that remark?" The slightest advantage with this mensch of a woman had to be seized.

"When I become anti-Semitic, Abe, you will be the first to know."

"Valerie, threatening me . . ."

She clapped a hand over her own mouth as if thereby to silence him. She spoke through her fingers. "I meant that the *Faculty Manual* is not Holy Writ. It was put together by mortals like ourselves. They could not have foreseen a case where the chancellor had to resign, not in these circumstances. Think of it, Abe. This institution is presently without a head."

"Does it really make any day-to-day difference?"

"Would you please consult the goddam *Faculty Manual* for a job description of the chancellor? This place will grind to a halt. Laplace should have named an acting chancellor before resigning."

"Maybe you should contact the governor."

Abe taught formal logic to small classes, refusing to lower his standards to the capacities of the average student. Logic is not for the masses and never has been. Nor is it any particular help in ordinary argumentation, any more than mathematics is. Nonetheless, he felt an odd exhilaration fencing with Valerie Kraft. He hated her on principle. She was a member of the administration and thus beneath contempt. The Herman theory of the university had it that the faculty itself should form the governing body of the place. Institutions of higher learning had been captured by functionaries who hadn't the least idea what went on in classrooms. To the administrator, the faculty is a body of pests, overpaid, underworked prima donnas who spent their excessive leisure second-guessing the administration. The unstated premise in this administrative outlook is that if only faculty and students would go away, the university could be run efficiently.

Abe did not know how much of this creed Valerie Kraft consciously subscribed to. It did not matter. The theory was built into her role and soon would be lodged, however unwittingly, in her breast. Where, he noted, there was ample room for many things to lodge. If only she had the milk of human kindness, he would have liked to lay his head on her bosom and explain to her that an administration distinct from the faculty is a comparatively recent aberration. Aberration. Was what was hinted about the vice-provost true?

He chased the thought away as unworthy of the situation. Besides, he must not humanize Valerie. His present task was clear. He must thwart her plan to find a replacement for the chancellor by having the steering committee of the Faculty Senate name a search committee. You would think that she herself aspired to succeed Laplace. The thought gave him pause. Was it possible? But what abomination was not possible in the present degenerate state of the academy?

"Now I know why it is called a steering committee," Valerie said. "You have no balls."

"As you pointed out, Valerie, you too are a member. You would make an odd eunuch."

"All eunuchs are odd."

"No confessions, please."

Valerie actually blushed. Valerie Kraft blushed. Had the truth been teased from a tense situation? No wonder Valerie hated him. After all, short, hirsute, threatening, he was a man.

He checked himself. Dear God, the fascinations of the slippery slope of fallacy. He must develop a course in informal logic, if only as personal therapy. He had a reputation for being the local stand-in for *reine Vernunft*. If his colleagues could glimpse the teeming chaos of his mind they would wrest from him the chairmanship of the steering committee.

Valerie rose and left his office without so much as a fare-thee-well. Coming to him had been calculated on her part; she had meant to disarm him, and thereby make him amenable to her demands. He had weathered the storm. What was it Saint Saul had said? He had fought the good fight. He had finished the race.

For perhaps two hours after her departure he lived in the illusion of victory. He taught a class in which, though he said it himself, he was brilliant. Inspired. Office hours followed, during which he was disponible, fatherly, a sure counselor. A bony girl whose overbite was being belatedly corrected had just left his office when Valerie appeared in the doorway.

"I have a solution," she announced.

"What is the problem?"

She closed her eyes for a moment. "The solution is that the steering committee *is* the search committee. We can pretty much do what we want to, as paragraph sixty-eight makes clear. That is why I here and now formally request a meeting of the steering committee."

2

Peter Kessel was converted to Ciceronian Stoicism during the years he was a graduate student in the classics, first at Chapel Hill, later at Princeton. If he hadn't thought Laplace would take it amiss he would have urged him to read the old orator's *De senectute*. There are ways of growing old gracefully, despite adversity, and Cicero had found them. Maybe Herb wasn't ready for the little treatise. Cicero expressed gratitude at having reached an age when he was no longer prey to temptations of the flesh. He was, at the time he wrote those words, ten years younger than the just-resigned chancellor of the Fort Elbow campus. Wilson of the campus police had it direct from the local constabulary that Herb had been at a massage parlor in Morton on the fateful night. Drunk as a lord, ten years older than Cicero, what had possessed him?

Kessel leaned over the basin in the chancellor's washroom and looked deeply into his own gray eyes. His soul looked back at him and it was the soul of a chancellor. He formed the words with his lips but did not say them aloud. *I want to be chancellor of this goddam university*. Caesar, that bastard, had been right. Better first here than second in the best university in the world. But Peter Kessel was second here, in Fort Elbow! No more. Bellini had spoken the magic words. He, Peter Kessel, was the senator's choice to succeed Laplace. The predictions of the Weird Sisters had had no more decisive effect on Macbeth. For the first time in his life Kessel truly understood that bloody play.

I would kill for it.

He spoke that sentence aloud while scarcely moving his lips. Then he laughed, ran a comb through his hair and poked at the dimple in his chin with his little finger. He heard his own laughter as he had heard himself speak those words, but it was the expression in his eyes that fascinated him. He really meant it. He would sweep away every obstacle in his path by whatever means in order to become the next chancellor.

In the chancellor's office, he tried out Herb's chair, some kind of lounge chair. That would have to go. Peter much preferred the steel and crushed leather motif in his adjoining office.

Enid buzzed to say Professor Herman had arrived.

"I'm in Laplace's office. Send him in here."

There was a pause, but he would bet Enid's expression had not changed. "Yes, sir."

Enid sent Abe through Kessel's office to the chancellor's. Peter was standing at the window looking out over the campus when Abe came in. From this vantage point at least the campus had the look of a place of higher learning. Students scurried along the walks, apparently in pursuit of knowledge. Abe cleared his throat.

Peter said, "So Valerie's giving you a hard time."

But when he turned to see the effect of his remark Abe was examining the bookshelves.

"I expected to find a complete set of *Reader's Digest Condensed Books*."

"I filled the shelves for him."

Peter liked the look of the books. Emerson, Thoreau, Fenimore Cooper, Mark Twain, Howells, Melville and Bret Harte. An American motif.

"They've never been read," Abe observed.

"I've read them all."

"I mean these copies."

"Have you read all the books in your office?"

Abe might have been a grocer, the way he looked over the top of his glasses and turned from the shelves. Well, his father *had* been a grocer. Peter's had been a salesman in a men's clothing store in Des Moines. He still was. Like politics, boxing and the police, higher education was a place for upward mobility.

"Let's go into my office."

"Valerie wants to be chancellor."

"She could do the job."

"Sure she could. But how?"

Crushed leather enveloped his bottom now. Kessel moved his palms over the cool steel arms of his chair until he touched their padded extremities. He smiled across his desk at Abe Herman. The secretary of the Faculty Senate was fully representative of the faculty in thinking that any member of the faculty could replace any administrator at the drop of a hat. To leave the classroom for administrative work was already a betrayal, a loss of a sense of purpose.

Peter had been through all that once and for all when he made the transition himself. The choice had been one between two species of power. He could have become one of a handful of eminent classicists. There had been no doubt of that; he had been assured of it by two of the four current superstars. But then he had imagined the thirty-year-long path that was being pointed out to him, the research, the papers to be written, the meetings and currying of favor, the politicking for the better positions as they fell open, finally landing on top. On top. What did that mean? Thirty years hence he would be advising some younger version of himself to do what he had done. That is the hidden lust of scholarship: to make a claim on the attention of future scholars, requiring them to read what one has written.

It had been, in its way, an epiphany. In imagination he lived out that career, exhausted its possibilities. Before he fully embarked on the scholarly life, he was bored by it.

What sadness he caused when he accepted the post as Laplace's assistant on this unheard-of campus!

"Fort Elbow?" Professor Irwin asked, her lower lip trembling. "Where is that?"

She did weep before it was over. He tried to explain to her the sense he had of the futility of a life of scholarship, but she was incapable of understanding such heresy. As it so often does, lying seemed the only kindness.

"It is because I myself could never produce four lines like those of Catullus."

He nodded at the framed script on her wall. The farewell of Catullus to his brother. *Ave atque vale*. Its final words seemed an appropriate sentiment. Her eyes filled with understanding, pushing away the tears. She nodded vigorously, a tragic expression on her thin, equine face.

Assistant to Laplace had been a first step.

Next was the chancellorship.

And then, in no more than five years, up the ladder to something else. Nathan Pusey had made the jump from Appleton, Wisconsin, to Harvard.

Now Peter steepled his fingers and looked across his desk at Abe Herman.

"What exactly does Valerie want?"

"She wants the Faculty Senate's steering committee to name a search committee or to designate itself the search committee for the next chancellor. And Valerie is a powerful figure in the senate."

"You think she would be the senate's candidate?"

"Or die trying. I've seen the look in her eyes; she wants that job." Abe pointed at the door through which they had come from Laplace's office.

"Would her candidacy be put to a vote by the entire faculty?"

Abe looked away. The question made his devotion to democracy wobble. Who knew what the faculty would do if given the chance of a veto? A referendum would be chaos. There would be write-ins. Anything might happen.

"I'd rather avoid that, Peter. The senate was elected to represent the faculty."

"So how would the senate act on Valerie's recommendation?"

"They'd turn it down."

"So there's your answer."

Perhaps. But that left Abe with an vice-provost scorned and a deep division in the senate.

"I think the senate should keep out of it," he said. "Who gives a damn what the faculty wants?"

"Not you, apparently."

"I resent that, Peter. My concern is that we not engage in a useless exercise in order to satisfy the whim and ambition of Valerie Kraft. Who do you think will be the next chancellor?"

"Who do *I* think?" Peter laid the tips of eight long fingers on his chest.

"Okay. Who does Bellini want?"

"Maybe you ought to ask him that."

"It could be you, Peter."

"Yes, it could." But any pleasure Peter might have taken in the remark was destroyed by the sardonic smile on Abe Herman's face.

3

Matthew Rogerson was nodding over Spinoza in a chair by his office window when the reporter from the student newspaper took his opened door as an invitation and came in. The toes of her sneakered feet met, her knees seemed to be arrested in the execution of the Charleston, her blond bangs formed a defense through which she looked at him with furtive shyness. She identified herself as Amanda Davis, eating the words as she said them.

"We're doing a story on the chancellor's resignation? I'm doing faculty reaction."

"Sit down. Use the desk chair. What have you got so far?"

She shuffled over to the chair, her self-consciousness painfully evident. Had she volunteered for this job as penance? More likely as therapy.

"I have to get used to people."

"Who told you that bunk?'"

"My counselor."

"Why would you listen to a lawyer?"

Her teeth were large and flawless; the smile dimpled her bunny cheeks. He could easily imagine her at the age of five or six.

"My counselor in Psychological Services."

"What is God's name is a psychological service?"

"I'm supposed to interview you."

"Go ahead."

"What do you think of the chancellor resigning?"

"It's long overdue."

The girl began to write and Rogerson felt a fleeting desire to keep her pencil moving.

"Wait. I take that back. Herb Laplace was a worthy successor to Wooley. Thanks to the efforts of them both, it will be easy to find the next chancellor."

He repeated it for her, rather liking the Delphic ambiguity.

"What does it mean?" Amanda asked.

"The acceleration of bodies on an inclined plane increases geometrically."

Her nose wrinkled nicely and she blew at her bangs. Her eyes were large and cerulean and less frightened now.

"What do you teach?"

"Idiots, mainly. Kids who make a mistake when registering."

"I mean, what's your subject?"

"Being as being, more or less."

"Do you talk like this in class?"

"Oh, much louder."

"What are you teaching this semester?"

He actually had to think. How the years blurred. He had been nearly forty years in the classroom. When he was young, he had known a great deal, but with age had come Socratic wisdom. He knew he knew little and he no longer tried to fool himself about that. He told Amanda Davis he was giving a course in Socratic wisdom.

"It's sort of a psychological service."

Her laughter was largely nasal. "How long have you been here?"

He was used to the look of incredulity when he answered that question. He could have taught Amanda's father. Maybe he had.

"He never went to college."

"Wise man."

"He wishes he had."

"So he could avail himself of Psychological Services?"

"I wish I hadn't mentioned that."

"Stay away from those charlatans. You'd do better reading the astrology column in the paper."

"I do already."

"Dear God."

"What's your sign?"

"Out to lunch."

"Your zodiac sign." Amanda was less nervous and shy now.

"I was born in February."

"Early or late?"

"Just in time for my birthday."

"Early in the month?"

"You can talk while you smile. Have you ever thought of television?"

"I'll bet you're Pisces."

"Scaly?"

"That's Libra. I'm Libra."

Marge had been Libra too. Is that why he liked this girl with the gerundive name? She reminded him a little of Marge when they were graduate students in Madison a million years ago. When he felt up to it, he would track their marriage from those early, more or less happy days in Wisconsin down the slope of the years, through the quarrels and fights until she finally decided to leave him. The kids were grown. She still had a chance at happiness. Happiness. The way she said it made him want to cry. She had gone off to Florida and a new beginning and within a month was dead, her car totaled on the Tamiami Trail. Did a similar fate await Amanda?

He turned away and lit a cigarette, repressing a shudder. The recurrence of types, of stories, of successes and failures, suggested a determinism he did not accept. The world had not grown less various. His imagination was weaker, that was all.

"How long have you been smoking?" There was shock in her voice.

"I started in the army."

"What war were you in?"

"The Punic."

"Did you ever see *Patton*?"

"As a matter of fact, I did."

"I thought George C. Scott was great."

He let it go. He had meant the real general. Is the general real? Philosophy 101.

"What have other professors been telling you?"

She had to think for a moment to remember why she had come. "They seem glad he quit."

"Happy he's out of a tough job?"

Amanda shook her head. "The ones I talked to were pretty mean. They don't like him at all."

"Would you like a cup of coffee?"

"Cigarettes and coffee too?" She was shocked.

"I also drink alcohol and generally misbehave. Laplace was a worthy chancellor of this university. Write that down too."

She did. "I forgot to ask your name."

He was tempted to tell her he was someone else, but he resisted.

"The only thing others liked is the fact he admitted what he did."

Rogerson groaned. A public confession of sins was becoming de rigueur in the antinomian society. Not that Herb was reluctant, not anymore. He had come by Rogerson's home the other day.

"This could be a godsend, Matt. Does the name Bancroft Danto mean anything to you?"

"You mean etymologically?"

Herb smiled tolerantly. "He got in touch with me the day after it happened." Less than a week ago, in other words, but Herb referred to it as a date on the liturgical calendar. As it happened, Rogerson had heard of Danto. A local product, famous for his inspirational seminars, Danto was much in demand around the country. He had telephoned Herb from Denver where he was leading a retreat for jaded CEO's.

"He begged me not to sign with anyone until we spoke."

Upon his return to Fort Elbow, Danto persuaded Herb that his public disgrace was an exploitable commodity. The script for a promotional cassette was being drafted, and there would be something more ambitious, an album, a series of inspirational talks with subliminal effects.

"The pitch is that I know whereof I speak. There will be a

direct-mail campaign aimed at high officers of colleges and universities who are under the same kind of pressure I was . . ."

Rogerson stopped him with a raised hand. "I'll wait for the movie."

"This has changed my life, Matt. I've thought about it and do you know what? There's always a reason. Nothing happens for nothing. Matt, I was meant to take this message to presidents, vice-presidents, provosts, deans."

"How about the faculty?"

Hordes of potential customers rose up before Herb's mind's eye, but he dismissed this as a distraction. "Maybe later. Right now I'm sticking to my peers."

"Like QE II?"

Herb's eyes lifted to the ceiling. "I speak with the authority of failure." He looked at Rogerson. "You know the source?"

"Do you?"

"Danto does. It's catchy, don't you think?"

"It sure is."

"Don't start, Matt. Lillie is with me on this. It's brought us closer together." Herb seemed on the verge of confiding the refueled intimacy of the Laplace marriage.

"Can Bellini get you off?"

"I don't care if he can. I am taking what I deserve. But it goes to show, doesn't it? I wonder what he had on Harrison. That bastard was going to let me off."

Herb wanted the notoriety of a trial now.

"You'll lose."

"That's the point. I'm counting on it. Mayhew tried to drop me but Harrison won't let him."

"You sound happy."

"I am! Remember how you used to knock my job, Matt? I resented it at the time, probably because at bottom I knew you were right."

"At bottom."

"It was a pain in the ass, that job, and I couldn't admit it. What else was there? Now I'm free." Herb wiped spittle from the corners of his mouth. "Matt, with Danto's help I'm going to make a bundle."

"Who will be the next chancellor?"

"Who cares? I feel sorry for the poor sonofabitch."

"Any guesses?"

"It could be anyone, Matt. You've heard the names. Or it might be someone else, someone no one has mentioned."

"Have you ever thought of writing legends for fortune cookies?"

"I've seen him on a talk show," Amanda was saying. "The chancellor. Laplace. I don't think I ever saw him before. Do you remember Watergate?"

"Don't you?"

"I was a baby."

Before you knew it, Ronald Reagan would be ancient history. Well, more ancient. Rogerson did not want to think how old he must seem to Amanda.

"What about Watergate?"

"Someone told me they all did that. The guilty ones. Wrote about it, told on one another, got religion."

Rogerson nodded. He found himself unwilling to provide even a halfhearted defense of Herb.

"Sign up for one of my classes," he said to Amanda when she rose to go.

"I don't have many electives left."

"What's your major?"

"Chemistry."

"Change it."

* * *

Herb called half an hour later. They were old buddies again. Herb called several times a day.

"Matt, come to my office. I need your advice."

"What office?"

"Have you already heard?"

"Heard what?"

"The same old office, Matt. Are you coming?"

Herb looked remarkably unchanged, supine in his lounger behind the big desk. The recently acquired and marketable humility had been replaced by his former pomposity.

"They want me to stay on as acting chancellor while the search for my successor goes on."

"Acting chancellor. Is this a drama school?"

"I haven't agreed yet."

"I always thought of you as acting chancellor. It made life tolerable."

"Matt, I resigned."

"I remember."

"They've finally remembered someone has to run this place. Bellini called. It's the first time I heard from him since . . ." On talk shows, Herb referred to the arrest in circumlocutions that suggested Paul on the road to Damascus. ". . . since I was arrested. Now he needs me."

"We all need you, Herb."

Herb's face flushed with pleasure. "It's good to be missed."

"There's no one to kick around anymore."

4

On balance, Valerie decided, she approved.

There had to be someone minding the store and the search for Laplace's successor did not promise to be quickly over. So who better than the discredited and resigned chancellor himself to go on doing what he had been doing until they could find someone competent for the job.

After all, what harm could he do? Valerie did not expect Herb to further her own cause nor did she want him to. His support could be the kiss of death.

"Then Peter's dead," Carlotta concluded.

They were having an early dinner—the senate met at eight—at an off-campus restaurant. Valerie felt frumpy and businesslike seated across from Carlotta, who might have floated in on a cloud. Full purple skirt, black blouse, her waist cinched by a huge patent leather belt with a silver buckle. These were work clothes?

"Just don't pump me about Peter," Carlotta had stipulated when she agreed to dinner.

That had been easy for Valerie to promise after her conversation with Mayhew. The lawyer was into his second Scotch before he got to the point.

"Bellini wants Kessel as chancellor."

"I'm not surprised."

"I am. Peter isn't thirty-five years old."

"Youth doesn't hurt. Neither does being a man."

Mayhew was chewing on ice. He swallowed and nodded his head. "You're a candidate too."

"I'd like to be chancellor, sure."

"You don't have a chance."

"We'll see."

Mayhew did some more chewing. "What do you know about Bellini?"

"Not much. Does anyone? He's a cement contractor with a lot of concrete experience. He ran for the legislature to protect his own interests. For some inscrutable reason he has appointed himself guardian angel of the Fort Elbow campus."

"It's in his district."

"So is the experimental farm."

"He never graduated from high school."

"That's the reason?"

"Reasons are usually bad."

"He's already received an honorary degree. I voted against it, by the way."

"Bellini remembers."

So much for the confidentiality of senate sessions. "How powerful is he?"

"His chief strength is that he knows no one else really gives a damn who's chancellor here."

"Do you?"

Mayhew waved down the waitress. "You want more wine, Valerie?"

Her glass was still half full. She had accepted it against her better judgment and already felt its effects. How could he pour down Scotch and go on talking? Did drink make him sympathetic with Bellini?

"Do I care who's the next chancellor? What I want is to avoid a battle. What would you take to give Peter a clear track?"

This was the first indication that they were at all worried about her. Did Mayhew know how much his question revealed?

"Are you speaking for him?"

Mayhew said nothing but the way he looked at her said he was.

"What's the offer?"

"Provost." He lifted his hand to still her laughter. "Maybe a new position. First vice-president in charge of academic affairs."

"I'd rather be provost."

"Okay."

"But I won't settle for it. I mean that. I want to be chancellor. I think I could do a better job than Peter Kessel. And I'll fight for it."

"You'll lose."

"That's twice you've said that."

"Lose not only the chancellorship but the vice-provostship as well."

Did he think she would stay on if she ran for the chancellorship and lost? She could see that Mayhew did not want to take her seriously. He would have liked to be amused by the thought of a woman aspiring to succeed Laplace. If she had been wavering—and she was not—Mayhew's probe would have given her new resolve. The bastards. They would find that Valerie Kraft meant business.

Not that she was unaffected by the reiterated prediction that she would lose. After meeting with Bellini she had sat down and began a list of those whose support she could count on. After a name or two, she put down her pen. She needed a dramatic weapon. She needed the media on her side. To begin with, the local press. And even the student newspaper, of which Carlotta was the faculty adviser. Hence this dinner.

"How well do you know the girl who did the piece on faculty reaction to Laplace's resignation?" Valerie asked.

"Amanda Davis? Not exactly a pillar of strength, but very intelligent."

Valerie thought the description might have fit her when she was an undergraduate. Beneath a phony veneer of sophistication, she had gaped in wonderment at the world and everyone in it. She had felt dumb, a country girl in a fast town, believing the worst of the other students while at the same time convinced they were as innocent as she was.

"She wrote a good article."

"Everybody liked it except me, I guess. She had no point of view from which to write it. I'm not sure she even knew who Laplace is. Or was."

"She quoted me accurately."

"You and Rogerson."

"Rogerson! Don't make me laugh."

"He certainly impressed Amanda. She wants to take a course from him."

It was a tempting diversion, to unload her pique on Rogerson and all he represented. He and Laplace were old warriors, vestiges of a surpassed phase of the school. Even granting Rogerson his charms (which she herself was impervious to), they were the charms of a throwback, a dinosaur. Valerie suspected that Rogerson himself knew this and in his own way accepted it. He would be no more preposterous as chancellor than Laplace. But she refused to be sidetracked.

"Let me tell you what I've been thinking."

Carlotta was attentive enough, but was she convinced? The idea was to link Kessel with the Laplace/Rogerson phase of the university's development and smother him with loving portraits of their quaint and irrelevant charms. Peter Kessel would be a victory for that Neanderthal past. Against that charge as background, Valerie could emerge as someone to lead the campus into the future.

"Look, Valerie, let me be frank. If there were an election and you and Peter were the candidates, what do you think the result would be?"

"He'd whip my ass."

"Of course he would. And if the election involved the whole faculty, not just the Faculty Senate, he'd still win."

Valerie nodded. The painful truth seemed neutralized by being expressed.

"I agree."

"Then what's the point?"

"Because that is not how it will be decided. No election is going to take place. The choice will be made in Columbus."

5

Of the eight members of the steering committee, Abe discounted two immediately, Handel and Valerie. Their votes would not be cast on the side of reason, Valerie's because of her ambition, Handel's out of a touching, not to say touched, loyalty to the woman who did his administrative work for him. Putting himself aside, Abe could discern in the five remaining no pattern Immanuel Kant would have been wowed by.

Kessel was for Kessel and so, Abe surmised, were the rest. Sylvia from Philosophy, Grossteste from History, Wiener from Economics and Barber from Art. The group had been carefully put together over the years, selected from those who despised meetings, came late if at all and would rubber-stamp anything to bring the agony to a merciful end. Abe had counted on this elite group to give short shrift to Valerie's intention that they should play a large, time-consuming and probably futile role in selecting the university's next chancellor.

"We would have to advertise, of course," Abe observed when a quorum had gathered twelve minutes after the scheduled opening of the meeting.

Valerie gave him a glacial smile. "Yes, we will have to advertise."

"Have you any idea how many replies we are likely to get to just a one-time, inch-high notice in the *Chronicle of Higher Education*?"

"We have all answered such ads," Valerie replied.

Barber stopped combing his beard with his fingers. He took offense at the suggestion that he would answer an ad. "They came to me," he huffed. "I did not go to them."

Sylvia said, "Personally, I was selected from a field of two dozen."

"And would be again," Weiner said, waggling his brows which represented the only hair on his head. His head was so bald that it made him seem a sort of flasher. He bowed when he spoke as if he meant for Sylvia to read his obscene thoughts through his exposed pate.

Kessel moved that they draft an ad and Abe brought out the draft he had prepared.

> Chancellor. Fort Elbow campus, University of Ohio. Four-year programs in humanities and sciences as well as pre-professional programs. Average enrollment of 12,000 over recent years. Outstanding faculty. First-rate plant. Bucolic location. Administrative experience in either business or academic world a must. Write: Chairman, Search Committee, etc.

"Bucolic?" Barber queried.

"How would you put it?"

"In English. What the hell does bucolic mean?"

"We wouldn't want a professor, let alone a chancellor, who didn't know," Handel said in a half-whisper.

"Chair*man*?" Valerie glanced at Abe, her raised brows looking as if they would never descend again.

The familiar wrangle followed. They settled for Chair. Thus did the realm of objects triumph over persons. But Abe Herman was pleased. They were discussing his draft without demur. In prospect was a flood of applications that would change the mood of the committee.

"I think we have two different tasks," Peter Kessel suggested when the proposed ad had received the kind of attention founding fathers lavish on constitutions. "There are in effect two searches, one outer, one inner."

"The inner is the outer," Sylvia said, then smiled apologetically. "Hegel?"

"How bucolic," Barber growled.

"An inner and an outer," Peter said again. "I suggest we proceed forthwith with the inner."

"An excellent idea," Valerie said, looking significantly at Handel. The provost did his duty.

"I would like to propose Dr. Kraft as our nominee. I have come to know her administrative talents and am convinced she will acquit herself with distinction as our next chancellor."

"I second that," Peter Kessel said. Valerie was astounded. She had been prepared for anything but gentlemanly condescension. Abe observed that Valerie Kraft's name was before them. Were there other nominations?

Peter Kessel was nominated by Barber.

6

It gave Laplace a posthumous feeling when he heard the news. Valerie and Kessel. But would any successor have seemed less preposterous? He regarded Peter as a protégé, a young man he had groomed for the job. This interpretation required stretching a fact or two and imagining an affection he did not feel. Peter's manner had always suggested a barely disguised condescension, but Herb had preferred to interpret the young man's manner as grudging admiration. From humble beginnings, Herbert Laplace had risen to the top of the heap, such as it was. How could that fail to impress Peter? But Valerie Kraft as chancellor? This was to remedy tragedy with farce. Imagine being succeeded by a woman.

The horror of it made it almost attractive. It would be a kind of proof of the general falling apart of things if he should turn the chancellorship over to a woman. Oswald Spengler would not have been surprised.

Spengler was one author Herb Laplace could genuinely claim to have read. He had added his own obviously much-read copy of *Decline of the West* to the props Peter had put on his office shelves. There was an odd satisfaction for Herb in knowing the world was going to hell, though he wasn't sure why.

"It makes mortality acceptable," Rogerson said.

Was Matt really less obnoxious now that he had returned to strong drink and tobacco? At least this ensured Herb of company in his last days in office, which he planned to enjoy in style.

Several times a week now, he and Matt saw the late September sun set from the office of the chancellor, chairs pulled to the window, glasses in hand, the air blue with smoke.

If nothing else, the sun was still declining in the west. "Like old times," Herb sighed contentedly.

"In what way?"

"A drink, talk, fellowship."

"You have me confused with someone else."

Herb ignored it, but Rogerson was right. They had never been that close. Now they were survivors, remnants of the past, drawn to a remembered experience.

"It was mourning Norah that did me in, Matt."

"Bullshit. You were just feeling sorry for yourself."

"And what were you doing?"

"Hmph. Who do you think it will be, Peter or Valerie?"

"You're in the senate."

"But not on the steering committee. Of course, no one has asked for the senate's recommendation."

"Why not Valerie?"

"Why not indeed. I'm told that Peter seconded her nomination."

"Did he?"

"I suppose that's confidential. Or it was. It's no surprise he would want her as his opponent. She hasn't a real friend in the senate, maybe not in the whole faculty."

"Handel."

Rogerson thought about it. "Maybe. But he would rather have her doing his work as provost."

7

Rogerson left before the brandy put the lights out in his head. The descent in the elevator made him queasy and he walked past the lot where he had left his car. He had no wish to follow Herb Laplace into the annals of local crime. He would pick up his car tomorrow. Answering Herb's requests to stop by for a late-afternoon drink had begun as a charitable act—accepting actually brought a little righteous tremor. But within weeks, Herb had made it penitential in another sense.

Tutored by Bancroft Danto but drawing as well on a lifetime of deviousness, Herb was quickly turning ignominy into celebrity. He had become the Good Thief. On local and Cleveland talk shows he had discoursed with phony fluency on the toll stress takes on top executives. He spoke of the perilous loneliness at the top, the fatal frequency of the offered drink.

"From top to topless," Rogerson said to the screen.

"The nation's business is conducted over glasses," Herb said sternly, peering at the camera. He might have been replying to Rogerson's remark. "You would be alarmed to learn how many government decisions, on city, state and national levels, are made by men and women whose minds are addled by booze. I have been told by literary friends that the same is true of book deals, movie deals. I do not have to be told what it is like for the chancellor of a university. He is a combination ambassador and salesman, he . . ."

Herb emerged as a victim of his job, a martyr to the pace he had set himself in order to be of service. A series of student editorials spoke savagely of Laplace's hypocrisy. Laplace took to quoting liberally from the attacks, agreeing with every word. There seemed nothing he could not turn to his own advantage.

His inspirational talk, "Love It or Leave It," available on audio- and videocassette, did well; Herb and Danto were now at work on an album. A series of seminars at motels across the nation was planned, with scads of local publicity and a hefty registration fee.

"Your strength is your weakness," Roger said.

"Is that Saint Paul?"

"No, Minneapolis."

"Guilt is big, Matt. And love. That was the best advice Danto gave me. You need love in the title."

"What does 'love it or leave it' mean in this context?"

Herb joined his palms and closed his eyes. "The idea is that, even though I was working my ass off, I had fallen out of love with my job. Hence the drinking. The trick is to work your ass off and love it."

"People pay to hear that?"

"I won't depress you by saying how much we plan to clear in the next six months."

Herb put on the cassette and Rogerson was surprised at the unction with which Herb delivered his message.

"You could have been a preacher, Herb."

"My mother wanted me to become a priest."

"My God!"

"I could have done it."

Leave it alone. Leave Herb alone too. Successful failure had made him more obnoxious than ever. Shuffling across campus to his office, Rogerson decided that the antics of the steering committee were little more uplifting.

"You probably think I'm for Valerie just because she's a woman," Sylvia said. She stood beside the desk in his office, hands on her hips, her great ripe body an undiscovered continent. Why didn't she get out of this life and get married? Of course, like all academic women she was affected by the pervasive feminism that made marriage seem a mark of failure.

"What are your other reasons?"

"I'm not for her at all."

"I think she'd make a good chancellor. But then I think Phyllis Diller would make a good chancellor of this place."

"Peter Kessel is no better."

"And no worse."

Sylvia sat in his easy chair as if she had just lost an argument with herself.

"How well do you know Valerie?" she asked.

"I hardly know her at all."

"I think she's queer. Can you imagine that becoming public?"

Rogerson grew uneasy. He had heard such things from

Herb, but then Herb assumed that any woman who spurned him was in the grip of unnatural vices. But Rogerson did not want to talk of such things seriously with Sylvia.

Once he had come within an ace of making an ass of himself with Sylvia, indeed he had committed adultery with her in his heart; but a fear of public shame had cleansed him of desire, and transformed Sylvia into a friend. He thought of her as his link with the junior faculty, a breed he viewed with very mixed emotions. The quality of the faculty had undeniably risen in recent years, but at what cost? Such calculating creatures these youngsters were, their minds abuzz with fringe benefits, teaching loads, the composition of tenure committees. Once people had wandered into teaching more or less by accident, scarcely believing you could earn a living at something so undemanding. There still clung to the profession signs of its clerical origins; it was a way of turning away from worldly pursuits. Let the rest of the world get rich, poor devils. We will talk of Plato to their children and earn our bread doing it. Now it was not just administrators who employed the jargon of the business world. Bottom lines and boats dead in the water and ducks all in a row—these and other tortured metaphors had trickled down from boardrooms and offices to the academy. For years Rogerson had felt squeezed between the administration, an old and familiar enemy, and the younger faculty, unionized, professionalized, always campaigning for more benefits and wages. Wages. They still called it their salary but in their hearts they were trade union members.

Sylvia represented the no less alarming sexual anomie of the young, which made her evident disapproval of Valerie's alleged deviance strange.

"Have you been the object of her sapphic advances?"

She seemed to have to think. "Not exactly."

Dear God. Rogerson in a stab at casualness shook a cigarette free from his package.

"If you're going to light that I'm leaving."

"If you're going to stay I'll smolder."

"I mean it."

Sylvia had a large *Ruega de no fumar* sign on her door. She had battled Right-to-Lifers at abortion clinics, she had fought the prudes who tried to stop Student Health from dispensing contraceptives, she was at least fitfully in favor of unilateral disarmament and to hell with the consequences, but she knew a menace when she saw one and was a tireless crusader against tobacco.

"How could it become public? Valerie's . . ." He was at a loss for words.

"Lifestyle? Because Peter Kessel will make it public."

"He plans to tell people what they think they already know?"

"It's the way it will be made to sound."

"Who told you this?"

"I promised not to tell."

Rogerson guessed Carlotta. Maybe even Valerie herself.

"I'll have a word with Peter."

She actually kissed him, but he turned his head and took it like a Christian on the cheek.

Chapter Three

1

Sylvia Woods was one of the charter members of Women's Studies and had been active in the program since its inauguration on the Fort Elbow campus. After half a dozen years, she still believed in the program, passionately, and was willing to give her all to overcome the systematic oppression of women that was built into our essentially patriarchal society.

"Matriarchal," Rogerson corrected. "Ask any European. They've known for years that women run this country."

"Is that why there's never been a woman president?"

"No woman ever ran for the job."

"That's false!"

"I mean on a major ticket."

"She couldn't get the nomination."

"What woman ever tried?"

"Shirley Chisholm."

"I forgot about her."

"Of course you did."

Rogerson seldom gave an inch. By all rights she should have hated him. But she loved hearing heresy from his lips. She could disagree with him on everything and somehow feel more affinity with him than with Peter and Laplace and Handel and all the wimps who championed Women's Studies as much as she did. There was condescension in their agreement whereas Rogerson, no matter his theory, treated her as an equal.

They had dinner together at least every two weeks and these occasions were far better than chats on campus, in his office or hers, or in the lounge. Sylvia would never have admitted it but she worried that the sisterhood would think she was letting it down by fraternizing with an old chauvinist like Rogerson.

"Sisterhood? Have you become a nun?"

"It is the antonym of brotherhood."

"I thought Robin Hood was." He sipped his Manhattan. Sylvia wasn't sure she liked it that he was drinking again. Laplace's fall had brought it on.

"Maybe Herb will talk you into taking the pledge."

"He drove me to drink."

"And drove himself to Morton. How about that?"

"What do you mean?"

"I would have thought Herb was over the hill."

Rogerson stirred in his chair and a once-familiar expression appeared like a palimpsest beneath his gray beard. Sylvia was glad that she and Matt were just friends, that it had never gone beyond that despite their one-time effort. How did she think of him? He was too old to be her brother, barely old enough to be her father, but she hated her father and she loved Matt. A colleague? How many colleagues did she not despise? Rogerson was everything she should not like—traditionalist, gallant, Catholic, against every social cause that stirred her blood.

"Massage is an expression of the male desire to be dominated."

"How old is Herb?"

"Biologically? My age."

"Sixty-one?"

Rogerson beamed. "Sixty-two."

"And still buffeted by concupiscence?"

"With men, the menopause refreshes."

She put her hand on his. "You're bragging."

"Peter Kessel was telling me of Cicero's work on old age."

"That bastard!"

"You sound like Cataline."

"Do you think Peter will become chancellor?"

"There are obvious impediments."

"Age?"

"I was thinking of his intelligence. Why does someone like Peter Kessel remain at Fort Elbow? Why do you, for that matter? Whatever the job market was a few years ago, it has improved."

"This is a stepping-stone for Peter."

For herself it had become a millstone. Life on this campus was pure politics. Being good at what you did was secondary to working the machinations of department politics and the antics of the senate. Not to mention the union.

Sylvia's thoughts about the union were ones she would not dare mention even in whispers. Matthew Rogerson was one of a handful of professors who had not joined the union. Not only that, he made public fun of it. Somehow he had survived the counterattack. It was rather difficult to argue that Matt Rogerson owed anything to the union. He said he would sue them if he did.

It had been three years since Sylvia had attended a national philosophical meeting and even then she had confined her attendance to the feminist sections. On the flight home it occurred to her that the sight of scholars from all over the country had intimidated her. The feminist symposia and sections had seemed a refuge, despite the ogling. There was no one she could admit that to, not even Matt. She developed the theory that Women's Studies represented a stage.

"When the goals are reached it will fade away."

"Ah."

"Like the civil-rights movement."

"And Black Studies?"

"They've endorsed Valerie."

"Did Peter put them up to that?"

"They wanted to show independence from the union."

The waiter asked if they wanted to order but Matt ordered another round of drinks. Sounds of a pianist desperately playing Golden Oldies fought their way through the thicket of conversation in the now-crowded restaurant. Matt hunched toward her, loving this.

"You are a Madame Defarge, Matt."

"Nonsense. But who wouldn't savor the situation? Herb Laplace engages in a drunken midnight race with the police after visiting a massage parlor. He is pressured into resigning against his will but within a week begged to stay on until a successor is found. Meanwhile, first the Faculty Senate, then the union and now Black Studies act as if the chancellorship were theirs to confer. I am surprised Women's Studies hasn't endorsed Valerie."

"Who told you?"

Matt groaned.

"And now there's the Bellini Committee."

"What's wrong with that?"

"Not a thing. The more the merrier."

"It's democracy you despise. Don't you think the people affected should choose their leader?"

"You do?"

"Of course I do."

"Despite our sinful social structures and the oppressive patriarchal and antifeminine bias built into them? Am I quoting you correctly?"

"We will overcome."

"It sounds as though you've come over." He opened the menu. "Shall we start with vichyssoise?"

His considered view was that the governor welcomed all the discussion and recommendations and particularly the dissension. The less agreement there was among the faculty, the more impotent they were, thus leaving freedom of choice to the politicians.

"I mean the professional politicians, of course."

"Matt, you're really not that cynical."

"We have not yet scratched the surface of my cynicism, my dear. The fundamental assumption of all this folderol is that it makes a difference who is chancellor of the University of Ohio at Fort Elbow. Think of it. We are now two weeks into our great crisis. Classes meet, students are filled with misinformation as before, payrolls are met, one cannot find a parking space, the ineffable student paper appears daily. If this episode proves anything it is the total unimportance of the chancellor. The job is ceremonial at best. It certainly does not interfere with Herb's entrepreneurial efforts."

"Did you write that letter for him?"

"Which of the twenty-six do you have in mind?"

"The letter to the editor of the *Tribune*."

"I'm offended. That was obviously the work of Danto, Herb's Svengali."

"To what depths will he descend?"

"I did like the remark about his obsessive machismo."

"That sonofabitch." Herb had usurped the feminist position, explaining his current contrition as an effort to get in touch with the feminine side of his soul.

By the time they left, the pianist was all too audible. As the night wore on, his playing became more vigorous and he moved into the less melodious part of his repertoire.

"He must be hard of hearing," Sylvia said when they rose to go.

"God is merciful," murmured Rogerson.

It was Sylvia's turn to drive. When she pulled up in front of Matt's house, she gave him a kiss on the cheek.

"Isn't it lonely living in that big house all by yourself?"

"It's haunted."

"I can believe it. What's that on your lawn?"

Rogerson got out of the car and walked through unraked leaves to the sign. The legend was visible in the beams of Sylvia's headlights. KESSEL FOR CHANCELLOR. Matt uprooted the sign and brought it back to the car. "A souvenir for you."

On the way home, Sylvia stopped and stuck the sign in Valerie's lawn.

2

Peter Kessel and Manuel Cerrado were a study in denim when they met in the office of the assistant to the chancellor. Peter's outfit had cost the better part of three hundred dollars, the fabric artificially aged as fake antiques are distressed by dealers. Cerrado's work shirt and trousers were from K-Mart at best and had faded honestly after many washings. The meeting had been arranged after lengthy negotiations. Cerrado had wanted Kessel to appear before a union committee and make a pitch for its endorsement.

Kessel had wavered and might have agreed if Bellini had not vetoed it.

"If you let them think they had anything to do with your getting the job, you'll never hear the end of them."

"I'll have to deal with them."

"That's my point."

Kessel had dealt with the union all along, Herb declining to have anything to do with those losers. The contracts had been worked out by Mayhew and himself, a painstaking business. Cerrado acted as the chief negotiator for the union. He wore the same proletarian frown now.

"What do you mean you don't want the union's endorsement?"

"I didn't say that."

"Do you want it?"

"Are you offering it?"

"You're not the candidate, Pete."

Kessel managed not to wince. He hated to be addressed as Pete. And in the mouth of Cerrado the diminutive sounded deliberately insolent. But then insolence was Cerrado's major weapon, that and the fiction that he stood in the vanguard of hundreds of incensed faculty and staff. Cerrado himself was employed in Maintenance. Sweeping all employees into the union had swollen its ranks and allegedly its clout, but it opened the possibility that had been realized when Cerrado emerged from the power plant as president of the union. The equalizing of the salaries of faculty and staff was variously described as the lowering of the former or the raising of the latter.

"Do you think it's wise for the union to get involved in management?"

"What do you mean?"

"Say this place were General Motors."

"Ha."

"Would the union involve itself in the selection of a new CEO?"

"They're AFL now."

"I didn't know that," Peter said. His eyes were drawn to his framed diploma on the wall. Doctor of Philosophy, summa cum laude. What had been his dreams the day that piece of paper had been put in his hands. His dissertation had dealt with the influence of Horace's *Ars poetica* on selected nineteenth-century figures. His father had found the topic completely irrelevant to anything he understood, and so indeed it was. That was its attraction. It was something good in itself. Useless, in the best sense of the term. Et cetera, et cetera. Those remembered arguments now struck his ear as they had once struck his father's. With the great difference that Peter would have given much to be the idealistic young man he had been rather than the calculating, ambitious bastard Cerrado clearly took him to be.

"We may not endorse anybody."

Peter nodded as at a sage remark.

"You're both members," Cerrado explained.

To his shame, Peter had joined the union. Valerie had as well. He did not blame her. Who but Rogerson would welcome pickets outside his classroom, invite them in, become friends with them even as he insulted them? Rogerson had assumed the pickets would be plumbers and carpenters, but he recognized them all as junior faculty members, except for Cerrado (whom Rogerson insultingly referred to as Cerveza).

"I see what you mean."

"That doesn't mean we don't want you both to know what the union expects from the new chancellor."

"You and I have no problem communicating."

Cerrado shrugged.

"How well do you know Professor Kraft, Manuel?"

"She never comes to the meetings."

"She's a busy woman."

Peter had convinced the union it would be inappropriate for the assistant to the chancellor to be privy to its deliberations and had thus escaped the boredom of those fortnightly get-togethers.

"We're all busy," Manuel said.

The myth was that they were all as burdened as Volga boatmen, dripping with honest sweat, criminally underpaid. Many faculty felt a romantic impulse to feel solidarity with the oppressed working classes and to fancy that their own sybaritic existence partook in some fashion of the supposed nobility of the proletariat. Daily evidence of the indolence of the staff did nothing to trouble this noble picture nor did a three-day week with an average of nine hours in the classroom cause doubt among the faculty that they were among the downtrodden of the earth.

"We're going to Columbus to see the governor."

Bellini had already told him. Cerrado would be received by a lesser aide, flattered, fed and sent on his way. Another element of make-believe. Why did he himself want to be chancellor? He had few illusions left about the job after being Laplace's assistant for three years. There was some pomp but little power.

"Peter, if I was your age I'd go back to the classroom. Nine hours a week!" Laplace had shaken his head. Every administrator was convinced that the faculty lived lives of pleasant insouciance. Peter thought so himself. Then why wasn't he discoursing on classical literature to the young, teaching what he had been prepared to teach? Because he had been robbed of his delusions. Latin literature in translation? Introductory Latin to a handful of ill-prepared locals? No thanks.

"I feel like Buridan's ass," he'd confessed to Laplace.

"Who's she?"

Dear God. The only one he could have an intelligent conversation with was Valerie and they weren't speaking. Carlotta? Up to a point. They discussed Russian literature in translation. There was always Matthew Rogerson, of course, but Herb seemed to have a monopoly on him of late.

"How's the campaign going?" he asked Laplace.

"I'm off to Salt Lake tomorrow. 'If Salt Lake Lose It's Savor.' That's my title. It was a crack of Rogerson's but I decided to use it. The title changes but it's the same talk."

"Is there much stress in Salt Lake?"

"How'd you like to be a Mormon?"

"What's it entail?"

Herb nudged him in the ribs. "They cut out polyandry."

"They don't drink, do they?"

"Are you sure?"

"I may be wrong."

"It's important. I'll have to alter my talk."

Laplace had given Kessel a copy of his inspirational talk on audiocassette, but it was still unplayed. Often when he came into Laplace's office, the chancellor's voice emerged from the corners of the room where the speakers stood, mournfully insisting on his turpitude. The penitent listened in his Barcalounger, eyes closed, fingers steepled. But Herb was an infrequent presence now and the chancellor's office was usually silent when Peter entered it.

Sitting behind the desk, as he did after Cerrado left, he felt no stir of his pulse. Peter Kessel, chancellor. It sounded all right until the thought continued. Chancellor of the Fort

Elbow campus of the University of Ohio. Was it a rung on the ladder of success or a dead end?

Such somber thoughts might have induced him to withdraw his name from consideration, but the image of Valerie Kraft seated at this desk restored his resolution.

3

Carlotta's course on the Tolstoy marriage, jointly listed in Modern Languages and Women's Studies, had not been the draw Valerie and Sylvia Woods had assured her it would be. Fourteen women and a dubious male had signed up but Sylvia sat in too and that kept Carlotta on her toes. Sylvia was fascinated and appalled by the relationship between the great Russian novelist and his wife Sophia.

"How many kids in all?"

"Over a dozen."

"My God. And he blamed her?"

Well, not exactly. He blamed the flesh, his own as well as hers. What he would have loved to be was a monk, but he wouldn't have lasted a week. Besides, he hated the Church. In the end, Tolstoy had to invent his own version of Christianity.

"She should have left him."

"She did have a sort of affair."

Carlotta was really not interested in choosing the side of the husband or wife. Was the Tolstoy marriage all that odd? Not among literary marriages, certainly, maybe not among marriages, period.

"Now you've got it," Sylvia said.

"Do away with marriage?"

"The way it's been, certainly."

Sylvia was far less convincing parroting the feminist line than Valerie. Carlotta's own parents got along fairly well. There had been quarrels and long silences but basically they had hung in there and now at least had one another as they walked the Florida beaches collecting the shells her mother filled glass lamp bases with for presents. Her father read Westerns and followed the Cubs on television. In late afternoon, they lined up with the other retirees to get into restaurants. What was wrong with that?

"Did you know Rogerson's wife?" Carlotta asked

"Not really."

"I heard she was a shrew."

"Matt's no prize."

"Did she leave him?"

"Yes."

In Valerie's version, Marge Rogerson was a brilliant woman who for years had lived in her husband's shadow and had finally decided to break free. Tragically, freedom had meant death as well.

"She waited too long," Valerie told Carlotta. "That's the lesson."

What woman wouldn't be stirred when Val got going on the plight of women through the ages? It was a melancholy tale of oppression and subjugation, with cruel and incompetent males lording it over their wives and daughters and concubines. But biology was the real enemy. Female passivity and male aggressiveness were aspects of the sex drive, but what was momentary pleasure for the man more often than not burdened the woman with the consequences. It was the enemy within, the womb, that had to be conquered—and so it had been, with contraception, abortion and lesbianism. Now a woman too could take her pleasure, seize the moment without dreading the future. Victory could be declared.

So why wasn't everybody happy?

Valerie wasn't. She was afraid of backsliding on the part of the converted, not herself, perhaps, but other women who could too easily drift back into the old habits of subservience.

"It's called nature," Rogerson, the old Catholic, said. "Girls want to be mommies. Men didn't invent that."

Finally, it seemed, you had to hate God.

"The male God," Filigree in Religious Studies said sternly. She wore bow ties and mannish shirts and her hair looked as if she had just blown in from Oz. God was a projection of the male principle, dominating, willful, omnipotent. It was all power. Read Feuerbach. "With a feminist twist."

Carlotta did not read Feuerbach but she hadn't been to Mass in years. Did Rogerson go?

"With trepidation. Have you been to the Newman chapel?"

"Is that where you go?"

"I meant it as a warning."

She went to see what he meant, going on Saturday night, figuring she could slip in anonymously and watch from the back of the chapel. For twenty minutes she wasn't sure whether it was a mass. Phil Floeck, the chaplain, seemed to be wearing an Indian blanket, and was the only male on the altar. Half a dozen women wore some sort of vestment and were indistinguishable from Floeck except for the Indian blanket. In the sanctuary, there was a half-moon of backless seats, and Floeck, flanked by his female cohorts, sat while other women took turns at the lectern. It didn't seem to be Scripture until Floeck himself read the Gospel. His feminine entourage stood at the altar with him during what used to be called the canon of the Mass. God knows what it was called in the Newman chapel. Carlotta slipped away.

That wasn't what going to church was supposed to be like. She wanted the smell of candles, poor lighting, pain in the knees as she knelt, the sense of God somehow all around and within her too. At night in bed she stared at the ceiling and wished she could pray.

Carlotta felt Valerie wanted to be chancellor because it represented power. Power? Was Herb Laplace powerful? The trouble with struggles is that you might win and find the prize wasn't worth all the trouble.

Where would she be ten years from now? On the ceiling above the bed, lights and shadows shifted in kaleidoscopic patterns. Would she ever be a mother? Did she want to be? In ten years she could be dead. She wouldn't be forty but she could be dead. Everybody could be dead. What Carlotta liked about the Tolstoys was that they wondered what their lives meant. They had been religious, too. Maybe she should convert to Orthodoxy.

Those were night thoughts. In the morning it seemed important again who would be the next chancellor. She had coffee with Peter and struggled against the thought that he was more plausible as Laplace's successor than Valerie.

"Now the students are getting into it," he said, handing her a cup of coffee. They were in his office.

"How so?"

He indicated the campus paper on the table before them but Carlotta did not pick it up.

"Tell me about it."

"Student government has appointed a committee to make a recommendation on the next chancellor."

"Who will they back?"

He shrugged. "It's becoming a joke."

"Becoming?"

"You've got a point. Valerie and I ought to talk it over."

"What's there to talk about?"

"I suppose the damage is done. The first mistake was bringing the senate into it."

"You seconded her nomination."

"The students," he said mournfully, shaking his head. "I would say the janitors will be next, but they're already represented by the union."

"I don't know why you're complaining. Everyone's for you."

"That's what bothers me."

4

It was with a valedictory eye that Matthew Rogerson looked at the campus and small Ohio city where he had spent his life. The scene of the crime.

When he had come to Fort Elbow it had been to his first teaching job, but it was his first in the same sense that Marge had been his first wife. First and only. While practicing what monks used to call stability of place, he had nonetheless always had the sense of improvising, of living in an interlude. We have here no lasting city? More like, this too will pass.

Cut it out. No need to play the mordant, unengaged observer with himself. The fact was he had from the beginning been glad to have this job and had never aspired to anything higher on the academic scale. What it came down to was that he loved to read—but what is called scholarship had always seemed the kiss of death to him. The attraction of English had been the chance to read full-time; its repulsion lay in having to listen to fey frauds foist increasingly improbable accounts of classics on their disinterested peers. Did anyone outside the ivied walls give a damn for criticism? Did anyone within?

"What difference does that make?" Ladrone, his fierce young colleague, demanded. "We're not in the Clifton Fadiman game." His stubby fingers each looked a section short but his thumb, bent back under the pressure of the opposite index finger, looked as if it might spring free to Jack Horner dimensions.

"I'm surprised you know him."

"In graduate school I did a paper on the Book-of-the-Month Club."

"Tell me about Foucault."

"Tell you about Foucault." Ladrone said these words as if he were decoding a message. "What in God's name does that mean?"

Foucault. Derrida. The apostles of deconstructionism. The slouching was over now, the monster had occupied Bethlehem and everywhere else, iconoclasm was the only remaining art form.

"Why should I care what people like that mean if their meaning is that we should not permit the author to occupy a position of prestige?"

Ladrone was more astounded now than he had been when Rogerson lit up a Pall Mall. "That's your idea of Foucault?"

Even the names seemed obscene. Maybe if your name was Foucault you'd want to give the finger to the world, maybe you'd have to. And mustn't a Derrida deride?

Rogerson had given up trying to tell himself that it was only age. The university and the world really were worse places than they had been a quarter of a century ago. Women wanted the literature of the race rewritten so it would not offend their ideological ears. Blacks spoke of the need to replace Homer and Shakespeare and Dante with classics from nonwhite cultures and did not like it when you asked for a list. Higher education was spread so thin that doctoral degrees papered over a surly illiteracy in everything but some particular pebble on the beach of knowledge. And the students, the students . . .

In the Student Center the television rooms were crowded with the devotees of the soaps, the steamy present-day analogue of the serial novel. Dickens would have cleaned up. Somebody ought to clean *them* up. Television and rock lyrics were the real teachers of the young. No wonder the courses veered wildly between frantic attempts to compete with show business and cabalistic mutterings meant to turn away the student.

So why couldn't he make up his mind about retiring at sixty-five? He had tried to make the case for it with Herb Laplace, but that was before the recent troubles.

"I have retired, Matt. I resigned. My life is in a new phase."

Herb even dressed differently, tutored by Bancroft Danto. Gone were the blazer, flannels and tasseled loafers of yore, the gray tweed jacket, the corduroy suit. Herb's new wardrobe had been acquired for his outside lectures and for the taping he was now doing in the same studio—now rented by Danto—where only a few weeks ago he had known the depths.

"Come along," Herb said when Rogerson looked in at the chancellor's office to find Herb just leaving, a picture in a four-hundred-dollar suit of funereal hue, the subdued paisley tie and the blue shirt adding a tasteful dash of color. "You can be my media adviser."

"I only read tea leaves."

They were driven to the studio in a car provided by Danto Associates. It would have been quicker to walk.

"They recognize me now, Matt. The students. It's not the same."

"Not safe?"

Herb laughed. "I should have played demolition derby with the police years ago. Last week I was cheered when I walked through the Student Center."

"You've become one of them."

"That's it."

Danto was a surprise. A tall man in Levi's and a dress shirt, open at the neck, sleeves rolled up, he had Amish-like chin whiskers and a spacy blue-eyed look that might have suggested idealism if one didn't know this was one of the most successful con men in America. When Herb told him who Rogerson was, Danto looked him over as if he might be another exploitable commodity.

"A professor?"

"Of sorts."

"Never heard of it."

Danto had brought in his own crew, and the student cameramen and other apprentices watched with appropriate awe as they swung into action. Herb did as he was told; watching him on a monitor, Rogerson thought his old enemy had the mien of a game-show host, the fixed gaze of an evangelist looking soulfully over the telephone number you could call to make your contribution, and the docility of a man who had spent his adult life in higher education.

He had to use his shoulder to get the great weighted door open and make his escape into what he would have liked to believe was the real world. Amanda Davis stood outside his door when he returned to his office.

"Writing another story?"

"I may quit the paper." Her eyes were intent on him, apparently to get his reaction.

"Congratulations."

"My counselor is mad about it. Angry."

"I'll speak to her."

"Him. Don't. He told me to stay away from you."

"Come in, come in. Tell me all about it."

She didn't sit down immediately but stood looking around the office. "It really is as messy as I remembered."

Messy? Perhaps. "What's your counselor's name?"

"He said you're Catholic."

"Did he?"

"Are you?"

"For my sins. I became one when I married."

"Your wife is Catholic?"

"My wife is playing a harp now, please God."

"Oh." She let a decent interval go by. "You mean she's dead?"

"That's right."

"I went to the Newman Club to talk to the priest there but he didn't seem to want to. They had just had a protest about Nicaragua and he kept shaking his head and saying the Church is the problem not the solution."

"Many priests speak with forked tongue nowadays."

"He said if I'm baptized, forget it. Just come to mass."

"Are you?"

"Baptized? I'm not sure. My counselor thinks you sent me to the priest."

"Good Lord. Corrupting youth. That's how they nailed Socrates."

He asked her how Chemistry was but she would not be deflected. Poor Amanda. She had come to college with the idea that there she would ponder the great questions, learn from the minds of the past. She wanted to know the meaning of life.

"They say I'm suicidal."

"Is that like being blond?"

When she laughed the vertical line between her brows went away. He told her about Camus. Whether to commit suicide is the first philosophical question. Any other question presupposes a negative answer to it. She listened so intently it bothered him a little. He switched to Pascal and told her about the memorial in which Pascal had recorded his conversion.

"That's what I'd do," she said fervently. "Write it down and carry it with me always. I wonder what it said."

He did not tell her how uninformative Pascal's account of his great experience was. But Amanda reminded him of the point of the life he led. Souls are immortal. He had believed that long before he met Marge, before he became a Catholic. He felt sure he would have believed that as a pagan. Socrates did. Persons may begin but they never end and what we do now determines what we will be forever.

It was the message of literature. What was Hecuba to him or he to Hecuba? Actors on a stage performing imaginary deeds are all of us, weighing good and evil in the balance of our souls.

"I signed up for your course in the spring."

Dante and Aquinas.

"Can I come talk with you?"

"If you promise not to commit suicide."

"I won't tell you what I was told would help me."

"Good."

"He said I needed a boyfriend."

"What's wrong with the one you have?"

"I don't have one."

"Write a letter of protest to the paper. Every woman student is supposed to be assigned a boyfriend at registration."

"I don't want one."

"Well, if you want to be happy, that's another thing."

When she left, he gave her a copy of the *Pensées* to read.

"I'm coming back."

"Anytime."

The lounge, the Faculty Club, everywhere one turned, were full of the search for the new chancellor. Rogerson listened darkly to the discussions, the union, the senate, student government, Black Studies, each wanting a champion in the post.

"I think it should be a handicapped person," Rogerson suggested and silence fell. There were thoughtful nods.

"Why do you say that?" Valerie Kraft, who was sound as a dollar, asked.

"It would solve the question of a parking space. No matter where the chancellor drove on campus, there would always be somewhere to park."

Later, Sylvia Woods asked him if he didn't really care who the next chancellor was.

"Just because you're close to retirement is no excuse."

"I'm thinking of staying on."

"All the more reason then."

"You might be right."

But the only prospect that pleased was a surprising one. Matthew Rogerson realized he would prefer it if Herb Laplace remained as chancellor. The known evil, and all that. Besides, the university deserved no better.

PART TWO

Rosy-Fingered Dawn

Chapter Four

1

Herb Laplace had been hurtled centrifugally from the Cleveland airport to all points of the compass, in and out, one-night stands, delivering his standard talk and, the next morning, being whisked to the airport and mailed back to Ohio.

The Atlanta airport, the St. Louis airport, the Denver airport, to say nothing of the infamous O'Hare, had become familiar places to him, stages with constantly shifting casts of characters dropping out of the clouds, changing planes, defying gravity again.

Laplace had done his share of flying over the years but nothing like this, and he had never really had a sense of the incessant activity in the sky. And it was global, not simply national. You brushed elbows with people who a few hours before were in Khartoum or Rome or Santiago. He began to feel the stress and tension which had begun as the imaginary theme of his speech.

Danto supplied the hosts with intros and Herb took the podium after having been described as a pariah. The drunken chancellor, the betrayer of his trust, the man who after years at the top ingloriously plummeted to the depths and was here to tell them how he had become unglued. The style of the talk was confiding, confessional, yet invited the collusion of his hearers. They were in the condition that had once been his. They ran the risk of public exposure even as he had. Here but for the grace of God go you.

"It wasn't the drinking that mattered or my pathetic effort to seek further oblivion in a massage parlor. Oh, I don't mean to minimize the sordidness of that night. But what happened then, however surprising both to me and to those who knew me, those who had worked with me, was as predictable as the sunrise. I was a bomb ticking toward detonation. When you put that kind of pressure on yourself, trying to give more than you have, something eventually must break. And what will break is you."

He thought of it as a kind of preaching. In hotel rooms, he often watched evangelists with the critical eye of one plying a similar trade. His talk offered a kind of religious solace, a conversion experience, but one that went light on guilt. He expected not belief, but credulity. It had been Danto's genius to combine an abject confession with a declaration of basic innocence. It was not the real Herb Laplace who had gone wrong but some surface self that had been foisted on him by the pressures of his job. His downfall had actually freed him from the burdens of that false self.

Herb came to believe this speech, came even to believe that he had written it. Bancroft Danto had run a draft by him, as he put it, even nodded in seeming acquiescence when Herb suggested a change or two. Had they been incorporated? Herb could no longer remember. It didn't matter. He had become the person the speech was about.

The greatest drawback of his speech was that no one offered him a drink. Only when he got safely back to the hotel and could ring Room Service could Laplace have the drink he craved, even as he emoted on the evils of alcohol.

But this reward was sometimes deferred if one of the insistent ladies who crowded the podium after the public questions agreed to stop by the hotel for a cup of coffee. Sometimes he risked it and suggested they have a drink, and twice one thing had led to another and he bedded the lady, both times unsure whose idea it had been. Maybe that was part of celebrity, becoming a sex object.

For a week after each time, Herb had sweated it out. He lived in dread of VD or herpes or—he found it difficult even to formulate the thought—AIDS. From seeming a romp, sex was becoming a minefield fraught with previously unheard-of dangers. Don't fool with Mother Nature. God, he sounded like Rogerson. Or like those films they showed in the army before you went on leave. Sex as contagion. Laplace imagined all kinds of consequences of these fleeting unions, once even went to a clinic for a checkup. Nothing. Had he worried like this in his promiscuous days?

Promiscuous? The arrangement with Norah had introduced order into his hanky-panky and he had been as likely to catch something from Norah as she'd been from him. Odd to think of her as dead.

From thirty-six thousand feet Laplace looked down at the piebald expanse of the Midwest and had a sense of the fleetingness of life. His normal terror of flying diminished when he considered that mortality was independent of altitude. Sixty-two years old, no matter how young he looked, and he had outlived all sorts of people. Norah. Marge Rogerson. Weren't men supposed to die before women? The land below seemed a vast cemetery concealing the bones of millions of predecessors.

Herb clamped the earphones onto his head and listened to the canned program of distraction the airline provided. What about getting a short version of his talk onto these airline tapes? He would have to suggest it to Danto.

"Good idea," Danto said, his head cocked to catch his own words. "I'll look into it."

"How long a run do you think I'll have?"

"You getting tired?"

"Not at these prices."

"Herb, you could step up the pace and give that same speech for five years or more. The fees vary, as you know, but there are thousands of organizations who need a speaker. What they want is uplift. And to feel superior to the speaker. Aristotle."

"What?"

"It's the essence of tragedy."

"Where did you go to school?"

"I spent a year at Illinois Tech. By spring I had a thriving pizza delivery service going. It's still going. One of my nephews runs it."

"How long have you been managing speakers?"

Danto's large liquid brown eyes gazed fondly at Laplace. "Herb, I've never had a client like you. I've had this idea for years and when I read of your troubles I knew the time had come. Ever look at these self-help books in stores?"

"No."

"There are magazines too. It's the new religion. People need to be conned into thinking they're better than they are. Or could be."

"They can be!" Herb said, the persona he assumed on the road now assuming him.

"Sure they can. And they want to hear it. Anyway, when I read about you it all fell into place. Maybe I wasn't completely up front but you're doing well, right?"

Danto had promoted fights, been vaguely associated with the World's Fair in New Orleans, represented several college athletes when they turned pro. Herb was confident that Danto was his ticket to independent wealth. Herb remembered Danto telling him of his stable of clients, of his travel bureau that made arrangements for nearly fifty speakers crisscrossing the country at all times.

"I would have liked it if you'd told me I was your first client."

"My first public penitent," Danto corrected. "By the way, get yourself an accountant and he can look at the books. I want you happy. This is your new career."

It would have been churlish to say he was bored. Five more years! My God. But he must be coining money. Danto had agreed to split what Herb earned into two streams, one of which would go to him at his home address, the other in the form of Treasury certificates into a safe-deposit box in Cleveland. His hedge against he knew not what. If anything happened to him, Lillie was the beneficiary so it wasn't as if he were cheating.

At the rate he was going, Danto mused, he should be able to salt fifty thousand away in Cleveland this year. Five times that plus interest . . . Sitting in his Barcalounger in the chancellor's office, the penitent returned from his profitable speaking engagements, Herb daydreamed of the independence that box in Cleveland represented. He would have to ask Danto to tack on a trip to Guadalajara or San Juan his next time out. He should try out the life of leisure and see how it suited him.

All this flying around had given him a new perspective on the Fort Elbow campus. For years his life had been absorbed in the place, it had been his world. But in the context of the vast nation he was seeing, Fort Elbow and the campus appeared for what they were. Previously he had measured himself against the other campuses of the state system. Now he returned to the intense politicking involved in the search for his successor with the objectivity of an alien.

"Herb, there are now five groups competing with the Faculty Senate's search committee." Peter Kessel stood at the window, a silhouette.

"Five? There's another?"

"A new group calling itself Independent Students has come out for Matt Rogerson."

Laplace laughed. Kessel stepped forward and became visible. "Sure it's funny. But it's making the whole process a farce."

"Who are the independent students?"

"A girl named Amanda Davis organized them."

"Organized independents. Rogerson would like that."

"I think he does."

"No!"

"He has issued a statement. It must be there on your desk. It appeared in the student newspaper."

Herb found the paper and saw the marked text. He frowned. "I can't read it. What language is this?"

"Esperanto. He suggests making it the official language of the university. To give English a deserved rest."

"What else?"

"Mandatory urinalysis and blood test at registration. Literacy tests for faculty. The equivalent of factory recalls after five years. On and on." Kessel was not amused.

"You can read that stuff?"

"The next issue, supplied a translation, but yes, I can make it out."

"Well, it's a free country."

"I've asked Bellini to exert pressure and get the appointment made. I hoped you would want to add your own urging."

"I'll see what I can do."

What he wanted to do was talk to Rogerson.

2

The purgative, illuminative and unitive ways represented for Handel the soul's intended trajectory, away from the things of this world, freeing itself by prayer and fasting, on into the inner self where contact could be made with the spiritual world. In class he drew elaborate maps of the soul's journey to God for openmouthed students who accepted him as the Rand-McNally of the spiritual life. The provost gloried in the knowledge he had of such figures as Hildegaard of Bingen. He was thoroughly acquainted with Richard of Saint Victor and Teresa of Avila as well, but his research did not extend to those figures. One summer in Salamanca, visiting the Casa de Santa Teresa, a convent where the saint had briefly lived, Handel had felt in palpable contact with the spiritual realm.

This made him act so strangely, Laura thought the sun had gotten to him and led him away to the Plaza Major for a soft drink. The sixteenth century lay all around them. He felt a contemporary of the saints who had lived here. At the local university they had once argued the status of the strange creatures encountered in the new world. Handel felt that he himself was being favorably appraised.

"These glasses are filthy," Laura said, sighting through hers across the plaza.

They were drinking Coca-Cola which, he assured her, was stronger than any bacteria, but she did not hear him. Laura never wore her hearing aid outside, claiming it magnified sound painfully and indiscriminately. Perhaps she was afraid noise would impair her hearing. She did not like the dark churches of Spain and statues covered with real clothing and apparently real jewels. When Handel lit a votive candle she stared at him in disbelief.

"Think of it as Lotto," he suggested.

"Gambling and superstition are two different things."

"Superstition is cheaper."

"What?"

"I couldn't agree more."

"How I hate this country."

Handel felt somewhat the same way once he was back in Fort Elbow. He hated himself as well. Provost of the university! It was vainglory, that's what it was, and imagine being proud of such a position. If Valerie Kraft did not take care of things, the office would not run at all and yet he bore the title, not she. He should have relinquished it to her long ago.

"And take a cut in pay?" Laura cried.

"Surely it wouldn't be much."

"Well, I don't want to find out. What's wrong with the job?"

He let the question go. It was not Laura's fault that he had allowed his vanity to draw him into the trivial tasks of the provost's office. What would his spiritual mentors make of a day spent dealing with complaints of sexual harassment, parking space requests, a committee from the faculty/staff union, an illiterate alumnus who had made a fortune and might conceivably endow some university endeavor? Without Valerie Kraft he would go mad.

Now Valerie aspired to higher things, to be chancellor, and she deserved it. Was that praise or condemnation? Handel shook his head sadly. What an old hypocrite he had become.

He could read in his favorite authors what a danger it was

to have mere curiosity about the life of the spirit. But for him it was a spectator sport. He became cranky without a constant supply of coffee during the day and in the evening it was either popcorn or ice cream before going to bed. A treat, he and Laura called it, and they were like little kids deciding which it would be. Maybe if they had had children their lives would have been different. But children had never come and Laura, without justification, treated him as if it were his fault. Perhaps it was. He wasn't sure he really wanted offspring. Was an intention to propagate necessary for fertility?

What he could not tell Laura was that the dreaded prospect had been realized. Laplace had called him in and after some circumlocution suggested that Handel might want to move up to chancellor.

"Dear God, no! I want only to return to the classroom."

"You never left it." Herb seemed surprised at the intensity of his reaction.

"I mean exclusively. I am no good as an administrator."

"Nonsense. You can hire someone like Valerie to take care of details. You might even want to retain Peter Kessel."

It was all Handel could do not to fall to his knees and plead with Laplace to stop this line of talk.

"You can see the circus we have, Handel. Everybody wants to pick my successor. We are being made to look like a pack of fools. You are the obvious choice."

He must actually have fainted. He came to on his back, lying in Laplace's lounge chair which was horizontal to the floor. Rose was holding up a glass and he had a vivid memory of Laura in the Plaza Major of Salamanca. The ceiling above him sparkled oddly and seemed to be descending upon him. Saint Teresa had been given a vision of the place in hell awaiting her if she did not respond to divine grace.

The office of the chancellor was vision enough of hell for Handel. He tried to get out of the chair but hands were laid upon him and a glass was lowered to his lips. He drank thirstily and then began to choke. There was alcohol in the drink. Someone tilted his legs to the floor and he leaned forward, eyes blurred with tears, choking while Herb Laplace beat him soundly on the back.

"I had to ask you, Handel," Herb said apologetically when the provost had regained control of himself, though his eyes still swam with tears.

"Why?"

"Do you want Valerie Kraft or Peter Kessel sitting in this office?"

"I don't care!"

"Don't you have any concern about the future of this institution?"

"What about Matthew Rogerson?"

"Rogerson!"

"His name has been mentioned."

"Do you know how old Rogerson is? He wants to retire after this year. He's been here forever." Laplace might have been describing himself.

"It doesn't have to be someone already here, does it?"

"Of course not."

"Well . . ." Handel's gesture was meant to suggest the millions of candidates beyond the walls. "I thought the search committee meant to advertise widely."

"They put a postage stamp in the *Chronicle*." Laplace's eyes drifted to the window. "I wonder what the response has been."

3

Reviewing the three weeks since Laplace's fall, Valerie found it difficult to discover what precisely had gone wrong. She was far from thinking that she could attribute any egregious mistake to herself, but it seemed childish to blame it all on bad luck. That night she poured herself a double Scotch, put on Sibelius and settled down in her study to try to figure out what had gone awry and why.

Her idea of pressuring Abe Herman to put the Faculty Senate in the forefront of the selection of a successor to Laplace had been a good one. Nothing that had happened made her think otherwise. She had overcome Abe's reluctance, the steering committee had been constituted as a search committee, and her name had been put forward as candidate for chancellor. The fact that Peter Kessel had seconded her nomination and then had been nominated himself did not diminish her satisfaction with the outcome of her initiative.

But then the union had gotten involved, quickly followed by Student Government, and then the campus paper began a series of truly silly editorials, the nonsense culminating in the formation of the Independent Students who wanted Matthew Rogerson. With this kind of chaos the politicians were in effect given carte blanche. What good did it do to insist that the voice of the campus must be attended to when such a cacophony was forthcoming?

This should have meant good news indeed for Peter Kessel but unless Valerie was very much mistaken Laplace's assistant was anything but confident of his chances. And what did it mean that Herb, Peter's boss, should have made an overture to Handel?

Carlotta had been absolutely no help at all in achieving some glimpse behind the façade Peter presented to Valerie.

"Val, I don't know. I haven't had a real talk with him in weeks."

"I am not asking you to break a confidence."

"There is no confidence."

"I understand."

On the other end of the line, Carlotta expelled breath. When she spoke again it was with exaggerated calm. "Valerie, if you want to know what Peter thinks, for the love of God ask him."

"Is he there?"

Carlotta hung up on her. Who could blame her? That had been unnecessary, Valerie knew it, but it told her how unraveled she herself had become. It was silly to blame Carlotta for the way things were going. Not that she had much confidence that the professor of Russian was in her corner. Carlotta was touchy enough where Peter was concerned. Valerie didn't believe for a minute that Carlotta was unaware of Peter Kessel's campaign. Did she aspire to become Mrs. Peter Kessel? Wife of the chancellor and professor as well, the best of both worlds.

But it was her approach to Bellini that had unnerved Valerie.

There wasn't a man on campus Valerie couldn't handle, but Bellini seemed of another species, not just another gender. She made an appointment with the secretary at the office the state senator maintained in the county courthouse, giving her name simply as Miss Valerie Kraft. Would he recognize the name? There was no way of telling when she was admitted to the inner office.

Bellini did not rise from the chair behind the desk. The room was blue with smoke and the stench of the cigar he held clenched in his teeth made Valerie want to spin on her heel and march out of there. It seemed a deliberate insult, smoking like that. His cold eyes seemed to study her reaction. He took the cigar from his mouth only to wave her to a chair. Did he always show such contempt for his constituents?

"Perhaps you know who I am."

"Who are you?"

"I am the vice-provost of UOFE."

"Yeah?"

"Second in command to Dr. Handel."

"I've met him."

He had met her as well, but she was damned if she would remind him and invite another insult. This visit was a mistake, she saw that now, but she had to go through with it.

"There is a great deal of interest on campus in the search for a new chancellor, Senator Bellini."

"What search?"

"I don't believe the choice has been made yet. Has it?"

"What do you think of Peter Kessel?"

After a pause, she spoke deliberately. "He is a promising young man."

"Will he make a good chancellor?"

"Someday, perhaps. After he is more experienced."

"He can acquire experience in the job."

"Peter Kessel is your choice then?"

"Who else is there?"

"Me."

She would have preferred it if he had laughed or gotten angry, said something, but he just looked at her, puffing more lethal clouds of smoke into the air between them.

"Would you mind putting out that cigar?" she burst out, deciding she had nothing to gain by acting out of character with this primitive.

"Yes."

"If you want to kill yourself, okay, but it is thoughtless to inflict your smoke on others."

"This is my office."

"You are a senator, I am a constituent . . ."

"Did you vote for me?"

"I can't believe this."

"What?"

"Do you only represent people who voted for you?"

"What do you want?"

Valerie stood. "I came here in the admittedly insane hope that we could discuss the next chancellor of the Fort Elbow campus."

"You want the job?"

"Yes."

"Sit down."

"Why?"

He put out his cigar. "So we can talk."

Valerie sat down. "Thank you."

"What you got against Peter Kessel?"

"I told you he is a very promising young man. *Young* man. He doesn't have the experience to be chancellor."

"He has been Laplace's assistant."

"That's true. It is his first administrative job."

"It's going to be Kessel."

"Doesn't it matter what the faculty think?"

"You mean you?"

"The Faculty Senate nominated me. Peter Kessel seconded my nomination."

He picked up the cigar and studied it. The smell was worse than when it had been burning. "It doesn't matter."

"What gives you the right to choose our chancellor?"

"The governor makes the appointment. Do you think he has the right?"

Valerie got up. "Thank you for putting out that awful cigar."

"I was finished with it."

He gave her the same fisheye with which he had greeted her. She was being dismissed. She would have given much to be able to think of some crushing remark on which to go but she stood there with her hands clenched, wanting more than anything to burst into angry tears. Maybe it was a victory of sorts that she got out of there without doing that.

Sipping Scotch in her study, Valerie welcomed an ignoble emotion. If she could not succeed Laplace, neither would Peter Kessel. Of course, one must fight someone with someone, with someone manifestly more qualified than anyone, herself included, currently on the scene.

The search committee must turn its attention seriously to off-campus candidates.

4

The Faculty Senate Ad Hoc Search Committee for a New Chancellor had met twice since the nominations of Valerie and Peter had been made. Meanwhile, the ad announcing the opening and inviting applications appeared in the *Chronicle of Higher Education* and soon mail began to flow into the postal box assigned to the senate at the campus post office.

The first two days, the box was jammed. The third day Abe Herman found a yellow slip instructing him to pick up his mail at the counter. A thin clerk whose hair was brushed back severely on his head heaved a bag onto the counter.

"What's going on?"

"Applications for chancellor."

"All these people want to come to Fort Elbow?" The narrow nose wrinkled. Perhaps, like many postal clerks, he dreamed of transferring to Florida or California.

Abe did not encourage the clerk in his discontent. He felt like Santa Claus lugging the bag out to his car but there was no merry ho-ho-ho on his lips then or later when he dumped the letters onto a table in his office. Opening the envelopes, let alone reading their contents, posed a practical problem of enormous proportions. He got on the phone and summoned the members of the search committee to an emergency meeting.

"I believed I warned about this," Valerie Kraft said with some satisfaction.

"You did," Grossteste said.

Joel Wiener wondered if they had any obligation to read the letters, thus precipitating a quarrel with Barber. Valerie and Handel whispered and Sylvia shrugged at Peter.

Valerie stood to command attention. "I volunteer to be a subcommittee in charge of processing and classifying the applications for the full committee. Fred Handel agrees that the staff of the provost's office can be used for this purpose."

Abe didn't like it, but he had no alternative, except for the suggestion that they hire help to do the job. But Valerie made him look silly.

"Quite apart from the confidentiality required, we don't want the usual sort of part-time people working on this, do we?" Valerie looked around disinterestedly. "Not that I am anxious to overload our office. Maybe Abe has the right idea."

"If he has another idea as to where we can get the money to pay part-time help."

Abe assured them the senate budget contained a line that could be used for this purpose. "Valerie and I will constitute the subcommittee suggested, if that is all right?"

After adjournment, Abe suggested to Valerie that they make use of the staff of the provost's office.

"Then why . . ." She stopped and made a face. "You don't trust me."

"I thought it would be unfitting for a candidate to have sole responsibility for processing the applications."

"Of course."

Abe had suspected the provost's office of everything but efficiency, but Basil devised a program on the computer, worked out a system for the opening and classifying of the letters and himself entered the data into the computer. The first report took two days but thereafter Basil had a daily update ready for distribution to the committee Monday through Friday. There was a total of seven hundred and sixty-seven applications before they tapered off, and these in response to an ad the size of a stamp. What would a legible notice have brought?

Most of them were classified as W's (wacko), the most improbable types who with varying degrees of illiteracy expressed their interest in running the Fort Elbow campus. The PW's (probably wacko) were sizable. Basil's refined list came to forty-eight applicants.

Abe felt that things were getting out of hand, but there seemed no plausible way he could tell the committee not to do its job. Its job? The ultimate truth was that they had no authority that was not self-assigned. They could express their preference but no one had any obligation to take it into account. Their assumption of the role had prompted others to do the same until the whole process had become a joke. And now they were faced with the task of interviewing forty-eight outsiders.

"We must make it clear to them that we are acting on our own authority," Abe said at the next meeting.

"That's obvious," said Valerie.

"I mean we should tell them that it is not our role to hire the next chancellor."

"But we can make a recommendation."

"So can the students."

"And the union," added Sylvia.

Valerie said, "We are what we are. We have run the ad we have run. These people have applied. I have proposed that we invite them to campus for an interview. Could we please have a vote?"

"Who is going to pay to bring them here?"

Abe looked at Valerie and Valerie looked back at him.

"Maybe you should talk to Senator Bellini. Or Mayhew."

Abe agreed to do that and report back to the committee. After adjournment, he shut himself in his office and told himself he should have gone into the grocery business like his father. He should have been an astronaut or an Israeli spy. Anything but this. The ad hoc committee had become an ad hoax.

5

Sylvia prepared lasagna in the microwave but the wine was a good Chianti and the garlic bread ran with melted butter. They ate in Rogerson's study, which was a study in chaos. On the wavering screen of the old black-and-white TV, a local news team were regaling one another with tales of woe and disaster.

"I will expect to be interviewed too," Rogerson said, wiping his lips with a paper napkin.

"That seems reasonable enough."

"I owe it to my constituent."

"Amanda?"

"My little gerundive."

"She never opens her mouth in Carlotta's Tolstoy class."

"Pretty good for a girl with bad sinuses."

Despite himself, Rogerson had been touched by Amanda Davis's quixotic campaign on his behalf. Rogerson for Chancellor! Dreams of Adolf. It would be only a matter of months before he was battened down in his bunker awaiting the final solution. Amanda was serious, however, and he reminded himself that she had been in the care of Psychological Services when they first met. He asked her if her counselor had suggested the campaign.

"For therapeutic purposes I am willing to do much. I am always at the service of Psychological Services."

"I don't go there anymore."

"Are you still reading your horoscope?"

"No."

"So you're cured."

Her bangs needed trimming. Hair got behind the lenses of her glasses and she seemed a feral child peering at him from the primeval forest. "You were right."

"About what?"

"There's nothing to cure."

"Did I say that?"

"Maybe not in words. I thought everybody else had it all together and I needed help because I didn't. But the premise was false."

"The premise was false?"

"I'm taking Professor Herman's logic course."

"Ah." Once or twice she had been in the back row of Rogerson's class. He thought of her as Eve just after the

Fall, wondering what had happened. He was involved in a complicated but to him persuasive argument, Aristotelian and Kierkegaardian in its provenance, that a life lived for pleasure is a life of despair.

"That's true," Amanda said when she referred to the class later.

"You found my argument sound?"

"I don't think I understood it. But the conclusion is true."

"That could be the case even if the argument were invalid."

"I know about the despair."

Confession time had arrived. What had driven her to Psychological Services was a breakup with a boy she had been living with for months. He was tired of her. He wasn't cruel or anything.

"He made it sound so natural. We had been all right for a time but now he felt we had reached a point where we should pass on to something new. We had become a routine. He was really sweet about it but still he was telling me to leave. When I did I took the garbage out and I felt like leaving myself on the curb too."

Who is so vulnerable as a rejected female? She sat in his office, peering at him through her bangs, her toes turned in, a puzzled imperfect child of the times. She was supposed to regard sex as superficial, something to be enjoyed solipsistically, the partner an instrument of pleasure. The act was selfcontained, partners could be replaced, what was her problem?

"Did you ever hear of babies?"

"Oh, we were careful."

"Careful not to get pregnant?"

"You mean did I think of that as a way to hold him?"

"Did you?"

She looked away. She was ashamed. To regard the use

of the reproductive organs as linked to reproduction was Neanderthal. Poor Amanda.

What was the difference between Laplace and Norah—or himself and Norah—and the kind of liaison Amanda had been involved in? The shenanigans seemed superficially the same; the difference was they were no longer thought of as shenanigans. Theory had trickled down into the lives of young people who would find the theory self-evident: sex is for pleasure, period.

"I wish we had had a fight about breaking up. But I wouldn't even let him see me cry."

What could these kids make of Othello, of Heathcliff and Cathy, of Paolo and Francesca? Rogerson had never felt so anachronistic.

"Your revenge is to make me chancellor?"

At the beginning of her smile, the tips of her teeth appeared in a comic way; but when her smile was full Rogerson was reminded of his kids when they were young.

"The counselor propositioned me."

"What?"

"He said doing it with someone else would cure me. He volunteered."

"Donating his body to science?"

The sound of her laughter enabled him to conceal his rage. What in the hell was going on in Psychological Services?

She changed the subject to the chancellor campaign. Did he have a platform? Amanda pulled out a cigarette. Was that new? He did not want to ask. "You can say that when I become chancellor I will punish all breaches of the Ten Commandments, and enforce on campus the state laws on drinking and fornication. Learning how to read will be strongly recommended as a condition of graduation."

"Could you write all that out?"

"Why?"

"I'll have it printed up and circulated."

Rogerson thought about it. Why not? My letter to the world, as the maid of Amherst put it. Rogerson's encyclical on modern manners and morals. What he put into Amanda's hands the following day was a florilegium of passages from the United Nations Declaration on Human Rights, several verses from the Sermon on the Mount and a paragraph or two from Kennedy's inaugural.

"You should get a VCR," Sylvia said. They had finished eating and were sipping the last of the Chianti. On television two lady cops were alternating hysterical weeping scenes with displays of karate. They looked caring when they fired their weapons.

"Does Psychological Services provide X-rated videos?"

"Forget about Psychological Services."

"I would rather make it a memory."

Sylvia took a book from the shelf beside her, leafed through it, put it back. She frowned at the spine. "Was Thomas Aquinas Jewish?"

"Why do you ask?"

"*Summa contra Gentiles*."

"His brother was a surgeon. Is there any wine left?"

When she left, she kissed him, a laying of her lips upon his cheek. He blew in her ear. Noblesse oblige.

6

The woodwork in the restaurant looked like yellow pine, stained dark; the walls were rough stucco; the lights a guide to navigation rather than illumination. Bellini sat in the corner of the booth and while he talked to Mayhew his eyes roved over the restaurant. The veal had been excellent. Mayhew was now eating spumoni.

"So it's all set," Bellini concluded, but it sounded like a question.

"If that's who the governor wants."

"I want you to talk to Kessel."

"Don't you want to give him the good news?"

"Have you talked with him lately?"

Mayhew had been keeping as far from the campus as he could. No one had sought the services of the university counsel and he had not offered them. The campus was a zoo. Once the chancellor matter was settled he would submit his resignation. He told Bellini he had not talked with Peter Kessel lately.

"He doesn't want anything done until the search committee reports."

"Does he think they will recommend him?"

Bellini was in shirt sleeves. He put his elbows on the table, finding room for them among the silver and glassware. "It doesn't matter who the committee recommends. They have no status. I don't give a damn whether they recommend Kessel or not. He's it."

It was clear that it was Peter Kessel Bellini had to persuade of this, not Mayhew. It was equally clear that the state senator wanted Mayhew to do the persuading.

"Talk to him," Bellini urged.

After those medallions of veal, how could he refuse?

He called on Herb Laplace first, almost surprised to find him in. Herb sat at his desk, frowning over some pages. He seemed happy to be distracted.

"Never go on the lecture circuit, Gil."

"I promise."

"Promise yourself, not me. It's hell. I feel like a yo-yo."

Herb glared at him. "Don't tell me you don't know what a yo-yo is."

"I could rock the cradle."

"Yeah? I couldn't make the damned thing sleep. I do better with audiences."

"Isn't it going well?"

"Gil, it wouldn't matter. I'm a one-shot artist. I don't expect to be asked back. I could shuffle my pages and read them in any order and still collect my fee."

"Which is high?"

Thinking of the fee revived Herb. "Imagine feeling sorry for myself because I have to fly around the country and talk about myself for scads of money."

"I had dinner with Bellini last night."

"I haven't seen him in weeks. I haven't seen anyone in weeks."

"They want to go ahead and appoint Peter Kessel."

"I know that. So why don't they?"

"He suggested I talk to Peter."

Laplace stared at him, then reached for his phone. He told Rose to have Peter come in. But five minutes went by and Peter did not appear. Frowning, Herb picked up the phone again.

"You gave him the message?"

Apparently Rose had.

"Well, call him again. Tell him I have the university counsel with me."

Peter was effusive in his apologies when he came in. "I was on the phone with Senator Bellini and I couldn't get away."

Mayhew said, "I had dinner with the senator last night. He's told you the good news?"

"Yes. He's an impatient man."

Laplace followed the conversation that followed in silence, but with obvious interest. Yes, Kessel knew that the governor wanted to announce his appointment. No, he did not think it wise. Far better to wait until the search committee had finished its deliberations. Yes, he knew that the search committee had no official status.

"What Bellini doesn't understand is that the next chancellor will have to deal with the faculty. If I were put in office in defiance of the faculty, what kind of life do you think I would have?"

"Never worry about the faculty," Herb intoned.

"I know you don't believe that, Herb."

"Forget about them. They never agree on anything."

"This is different. They may differ on candidates but not on their right to nominate someone."

"Don't you want to be chancellor?"

Peter looked at Herb, then back at Mayhew. "Of course."

"You don't sound enthusiastic," said Herb.

"Ask Herb if he was enthusiastic when he got the job," said Mayhew.

"You're damn right I was. I like this job. Peter, you're a fool to cater to the Faculty Senate."

"Then I'm a fool."

"Well, that's settled." But Laplace smiled when he said it. "Gil, does Bellini know Rogerson's a candidate?"

"He's too old," Mayhew said.

"Among other impediments," Peter added.

"He's not so old," Herb said in an oddly subdued voice.

"What have you done with your hair, Herb?" Kessel asked. When the sunlight from the window struck it Herb's hair had a mahogany appearance.

"Nothing."

"It looks darker."

"He's dyeing it," Peter said when Mayhew went on to the assistant to the chancellor's office. "Bancroft Danto is rebuilding Herb."

"He's certainly come through adversity with flying colors."

"And thumbing his nose."

"He seems reconciled to leaving here."

"I almost envy him," Peter said, waving Mayhew to a chair. "Now that his job is in reach I think of all kinds of reasons I don't want it."

"So you are stalling?"

"Only in part. I meant it about the faculty. They have to have their say."

Chapter Five

1

Abe Herman had brought the search committee to an impasse, preventing either Peter or Valerie from commanding a majority of votes. The deed would have been impossible without the indolence and vanity of the members of the committee, his own manipulative skills and, of course, the doomed efforts of the two candidates themselves.

Barber from Art, his ascot tugged to one side of his turkey throat, thinning hair wild on his head, was more than eager to sell his soul but unsure what the traffic would bear. Like Buridan's ass he could not decide between equal piles of hay equidistant from him. Valerie's failure to bid brazenly for his vote convinced Abe that she was deeper and more cunning than Kessel and he waited for her to make her offer clear.

Grossteste wearied the other members with supposed historical parallels to their plight, their deliberations, their quarrels.

"What is the historical origin of the phrase 'pain in the ass'?" Joel Wiener asked him sweetly.

"I'll have to look it up."

"Good."

Handel was for Valerie, for reasons he confided to Abe but would not publicly voice.

"If we put Peter in, Valerie will put the screws on him and he will bend over backward to placate her. The union, Black Studies, everyone will descend on him and he will try to please them all. It can't be done. We don't want someone to broker the various power groups. Valerie is the kind of feminist who claims moral ascendancy over other oppressed groups. She will be less in hock than Peter."

Wiener was for Peter.

"To keep him quiet," Sylvia Woods suggested. "Peter saw Wiener in Cleveland wearing a toupee."

"So what?"

She looked at him for a moment, then lifted Abe's hand and pointed at the hair sprouting from the backs of his fingers.

"How can you feel really bald with hands like those?"

Sylvia was uncommitted, or at least noncommittal. Valerie assumed she had her vote and so did Peter Kessel, and Sylvia had contributed nothing to the pointless discussion of outside candidates. The forty-eight hopefuls would be sent a letter after the appointment was made. Abe only hoped none of them would sue. Sylvia had managed to attend every meeting of the committee without revealing the way her vote would go.

The immobilization of the search committee had been at first an end in itself, done for the sheer satisfaction of proving to himself the power he had over this creature of his own making. To thwart the ambition of others always seemed a contribution to the common good, but in the smithy of his soul Abe Heman did not have to forge altruistic reasons for his actions.

Valerie represented the menace of the new woman, demanding, asserting her rights, justice forever on her lips, but at bottom, using the rhetoric of women's rights for her own advantage, conning other women and cowing men into doing what she wanted. As chancellor, she would be a harridan, the university would become her toy, the systematic deballing of the place and of everyone in it would be accelerated. Besides, deep down in his heart, Abe felt she despised him. He was a swarthy denizen of Middle Eastern bazaars, a refugee from Eastern Europe, not really part of the caste. There would be no quota for those opposed to quotas. Stopping Valerie was manifestly in his self-interest.

Peter? God help us. If there were brains in that well-shaped head, thoughts behind those serene and caring eyes, if Peter was, as claimed, one of the most promising young classicists of the past ten years, deep questions arose. First, the most embarrassing of all, if he was that good what in hell was he doing on the Fort Elbow campus of the University of Ohio?

"There are no jobs in classics," Carlotta said when he had raised the question obliquely over coffee.

"Not even for the most promising young scholar of his generation?"

"He could have stayed at Princeton but not on a tenure track. The same at Chapel Hill. If he had wanted a prestigious address, he could have had it, but it would have been temporary."

"Fort Elbow is forever?"

"God forbid." Carlotta rolled her eyes. It was mandatory to speak of this campus as impossibly infra dig. The town was a backwater, the students marginal and one's colleagues, well . . . Did Carlotta really believe she was meant for something better? It was clear she thought Peter was.

It made Abe uneasy that he felt the same way. Peter made

him nervous. He didn't belong here and whenever Abe spoke to him he felt he had been called from the caddie shack to speak to the member's son whose bag of clubs he was about to haul around the undulating course of the Minnekada Golf Club. Peter had a built-in condescension, an effortless and unstated superiority to his surroundings—and the fact that he never voiced it made it all the more authoritative, at least to Abe Herman. Others might say they just liked Kessel, that he was honest and fair, that he would look good as chancellor and be good, besides. But for Abe, to vote for Peter would be to acquiesce in the feelings of native inferiority Peter brought on.

Such thoughts scarcely formed in his mind let alone escaped his lips, but the upshot was, quite apart from the fun of playing the committee like a musical instrument of his own devising, that Abe Herman was against both local candidates before the committee.

Who, then?

Abe shaved with an electric razor, largely because he had to shave more than once a day and it was easy to use an electric razor in his office. Moreover, in the morning, he could move around his apartment doing other things while he ran his cordless razor over his face. It was not until the search committee was formed that he realized there was another reason. He did not have to face himself in the mirror each morning.

It was his father who dwelt over the sink in his bathroom. If Abe Junior looked into the mirror, increasingly it was Abe Senior who looked out, and seeing his father in himself Abe was filled with ambivalent feelings. His parents had worked twelve hours a day, six days a week in the store, filling orders, running charge accounts, delivering. His mother was there almost as much as his father. They belonged to that store more surely than a lifer belonged to his prison, yet how proud they had been of their business, their customers, their independence. But they had been determined their son would go on to better things. Sandy, the daughter? She married a loser from North Minneapolis who failed in business at least once every year and a half.

Abe's features, the set of his shoulders, the lopsided smile and the goddam elephantine ears, were his father's. It was like a horror movie. The hero's face crumbles before our eyes and soon there is revealed the underlying monster. Not that he thought of his father as a monster, God forbid. But the physical reemergence of the South Minneapolis grocer seemed an ironic comment on his supposed rising to better things.

Now, though, Abe Herman saw something new when he looked in the mirror and this new sight pleased him. He saw the next chancellor of the Fort Elbow campus.

2

Sylvia Woods was five feet eleven, one hundred and forty pounds, a knockout in the swimming suit in which she swam each day in the university pool, thirty-seven years old, a tenured member of the Philosophy Department, twice recipient of the Best Teacher Award, author of an article on acts of omission soon to appear in the *Journal of Process Philosophy*, and bored to tears.

Well, maybe not tears. More like a vast suppressed yawn.

Her mother would eye her over the rim of her drink on their semiannual reunion and ask who the man in her life was. What she meant was Sylvia ought to get married, something her mother had done three times. Sylvia had mocked this suggestion for years, to her mother, in the homes of well-meaning friends, in the privacy of her own apartment.

Lately it occurred to her that even if her mother was right, the matter was increasingly academic. After all, she was not beating men away from her door, turning down proposals of marriage, fighting to remain single. Was her present condition a choice or simply fate? In what sense had she not married?

Such thoughts led to her paper on acts of omission. How can we be held responsible for what we do not do? There is an infinity of acts I do not perform. I cannot perform them all, perhaps, but I could perform any of them. If I am responsible for those I do not do, I am overwhelmingly guilty.

"Good question," Rogerson said, pulling the white plastic strip that opened a fresh package of cigarettes. Sometimes Sylvia thought he smoked only when they were together.

"Got any good answers?"

"Does the distinction between negation and privation mean anything to you?"

"How does it apply to the fact that I have not married?"

"You tell me."

She got him off that and he went on with the example of his own not being the chief rabbi of Antioch. Rogerson was genuine fun. He despised analytic philosophy, saying he preferred Scrabble. Arguing with him was never just debating. And she liked his examples. After their first exchange on acts of omission, Sylvia had read *Lord Jim* for the first time.

If she were to answer her mother's question as to who the man in her life was, she might have said Matt Rogerson.

Why they got along so well mystified her. He was a repository of outlandish beliefs and practices. Not long ago he had assured her that he went to confession at least four times a year. Sylvia could not believe it. It had been her understanding that even Catholics had gotten over such stuff. And Rogerson had become a Catholic to marry the wife who was now dead.

"Can't you give it up now?"

"Till death do us part?"

"Why not?"

He studied the ash of his cigarette. When he looked at her, he was smiling but his eyes were serious. "Because I believe it all, Sylvia, every jot and tittle."

A little silence, soon relieved by his asking if she knew what a tittle was. Personally, he liked people with big tittles. Were all serious people comic?

Quite apart from his theological beliefs (which Sylvia did not pretend to understand), his moral philosophy, his politics, his attitude toward everything that really mattered to her, well, he was outrageous all around. And he continued to surprise her. It now turned out that he was actually opposed to contraceptives.

"Matt!"

"I've shocked you."

"You're not serious, are you?"

Amanda had quoted Rogerson to the effect that it was scandalous that Student Health provided information on contraception and the requisite equipment.

"As serious as Huxley in *Brave New World*."

Another book she hadn't read, but she was not to be intimidated. "Matt, kids are going to do it. You claim you're against abortion."

"Claim?"

"Okay, you're against abortion. So you ought to be against unwanted children."

"Non sequitur, my dear. I am against sexual activity on the part of those who are unprepared to accept it for what it is."

"And what is it?"

"A way of making babies. The way the species is preserved."

"My God."

"That is not a theory, Sylvia. It is simple fact."

"Biological fact!"

"You're sneering."

"It's that goddam cigarette smoke. Why do you smoke if . . ."

Oh, the hell with it. It was easier to think he didn't really believe these things. She realized that it was stimulating to discuss such things with him, and not just intellectually.

Did she like Rogerson in a beard? It made him look older, perhaps, or maybe it would be truer to say it made him look his age. Without it he might still be in his fifties. But he was as old as her father would have been.

"What would you do if you were chancellor, I wonder."

A dreamy look came into his eyes and he took an enormous drag on his cigarette. "Resign, I suppose. But I wouldn't mind a month of it. Make that a week. One could do a lot in a week."

"Have you read the *Faculty Manual* Matt? The chancellor has very little power."

"Is that why Valerie and Kessel want the job?"

"They're more diplomatic than you are."

"More sins of omission."

What you had to grant Rogerson was consistency. If extramarital sex was wrong, then it was wrong of Student Health to pass out contraceptives. Only an idiot would deny that was an acceptance of extramarital sex. Do it but don't get pregnant, that was the message. But kids kept on getting pregnant and Student Health also made abortion referrals. Meaning they did everything but set up the appointment.

That way a girl wasn't trapped by her mistake, by a baby, by her partner of the moment. Rogerson scoffed at calling this responsible.

"That's like calling bulimia responsible eating. Eat all you want, but don't get fat."

"Do you really think things were better when sex was illegal?"

"Things?"

"People."

"Are people better now?"

"At least they don't have a lot of crazy fears and hangups."

"Then why is more and more sex education still the crying need of the time?"

You never won an argument with Rogerson. Not that Sylvia thought she lost either. Rogerson was the past, with all its charms, maybe, but the past nonetheless. He just didn't fit in the present time. And she told him so.

"Sylvia, that is the nicest thing you've ever said to me."

3

Lillie Laplace's idea of a debauch had always been two cups of nondecaffeinated coffee and wiping out half a layer of a Whitman Sampler. Rogerson couldn't remember ever seeing her drink before. But here she was swilling beer and blubbering and he couldn't figure out whether to try to talk to her or not.

She had called the night before and asked him to come to the house today at four. For tea.

"Whatchamacallit is on the road, of course."

"I wouldn't have come if I thought otherwise."

Forget the jokes. Lillie was afloat on a sea of suds, which in her case might have meant a couple of bottles.

"You promised me tea," he said when she offered him a beer.

"I hate tea."

"Coffee?"

"There's only the pot I made this morning."

Rogerson ended up with a diet drink that made his mouth as dry and wooly as a hangover. There were various warnings on the can he chose not to read.

"Herb's on the road," he repeated.

"In the air. Talk, talk, talk. Not to me. To people all across the country. Imagine! All his life he's been trying to hide what a shit he is and here it turns out to be his fortune."

"He'll be able to retire."

"And hang around the house all day? Not on your life. I want him to go on working."

"When does he leave office?"

She had to think about it. Her mouth became slack. Did she realize Herb was no longer chancellor?

"When do you think they'll appoint a new chancellor?"

"I'm surprised it's taken so long."

"The nerve, asking Herb to stay on until they do."

"I'm glad he did."

"What's he going to do when he runs out of people to lecture to?"

"You can move to Florida."

She made a face. "You ever been to Florida?"

The last time he had been was when he went down to claim the body of his wife.

"Sissy used to live in St. Pete." Sissy was her daughter, now in San Diego. "Visit her anytime but the dead of winter and you'd see what I mean. All summer they live inside, like frozen food."

"Felix Freeman likes Arizona."

"Felix Freeman." Lillie shook her head. "I'd almost forgotten him."

Felix had come for Marge's funeral but he had avoided Herb Laplace, so Lillie wouldn't have seen him either. Actually, Felix had had nothing but trouble with the desert retirement home he had bought on the strength of a glossy brochure. But then Felix would complain about heaven when he got there.

"If Marge were still alive I would have called her," Lillie Laplace said, hoisting herself to her feet. "I have to talk to someone."

"Go ahead."

"You'll take Herb's side."

Herbicide? Maybe he would. "I'll be impartial."

"I'll bet." Lillie left the room after tugging up her grayish slacks and tugging down her big baggy sweater. She came back from the kitchen with another beer, rolling from side to side like a linebacker. She stopped and looked down at Rogerson. "Did you mean what you said about Norah Vlach?"

"Every word. What did I say?"

"That you and everyone else fooled around with her?"

"Did I say that?"

"I thought you were lying."

"With Norah? What difference does it make now?"

"He's still at it."

Herb. Did she care? That pathetic drive to the massage parlor in Morton summed up Herb's sex life. It was all beneath the belt; it had nothing to do with anything beside its momentary self. Lillie should know that.

"Bancroft Danto won't let me go along on these trips."

"They can't be much fun."

"Ha! Herb's having fun, you can bet on that."

"Confessing his faults?"

"Adding to them." She looked at him significantly. "I know."

"Wives always know. What's Danto like?"

"He's a hustler."

"I know that."

"I only met him once. And I've talked to him on the phone. He told me the image of Herb arriving alone and leaving alone was better for the lecture tour. But he isn't alone all the time."

"No man is an island."

"You've heard the speech. That's Herb's line."

"I'll remember that. Have you heard the speech?"

Her eyes rolled heavenward. "Have I heard the speech. Live, on tape, in my sleep. He likes to put on the tape when he's home. He says it helps him on the road."

"I hope you're saving the money."

"Money. Where is it?"

She felt she was losing Herb, that was the problem. Most of her married life she thought she would have cheerfully kicked him out and now she couldn't hold him.

"Look at me," she cried, opening her arms. Rogerson was reminded of a gunnysack full of footballs. Poor Lillie. Being puffed up didn't fill her with pride and some sadistic hairdresser had turned her hair into a kind of Caucasian Afro. Her bloodshot eyes studied his reaction.

"We're all older, Lillie."

"Women are older than men. They look older. They don't age well."

Was that true? Rogerson doubted it. He knew women in their sixties he would run away with if asked.

"You look younger than Herb."

"And you're a liar." But she liked hearing it anyway. She shifted her weight on the couch. "I'm going to try hypnotism."

"What for?"

"To lose weight."

"Does it work?"

"I'll try anything."

"Why not just go on a diet?"

She looked at him as Sylvia did when they talked about sex.

"Just like that. Have you ever had a weight problem?"

Right now his problem was lifting his weight off this chair and getting out of there. Whatever Lillie's grievances, they were so all-encompassing he did not know what to tell her. He got to his feet.

"Hang in there, Lillie."

"I wish Herb hadn't resigned. He didn't have to. He's brazen enough to have gotten through it. Matt, I really don't know what will become of us."

He sat beside her and put his arm around her. Well, not quite around her. There was even more to Lillie than met the eye.

"Marge went to Weight Watchers for a while."

"And now she's dead."

"I don't think there's a causal connection."

"I mean, what difference does it make now?"

He went out to his car with Wordsworth going in his head. *But now she's in her grave, and, oh,/The difference to me*.

4

Carlotta liked Peter better now that the prospect of actually being named chancellor had forced him to ask himself if he wanted the job.

"I have no illusions, Carlotta. I've been privy to what goes on in that office. All a chancellor does is watch other people run the university. They don't know they are really in charge and he doesn't tell them, of course, but that's the way it really is. Look at the way things are now. Herb is gone three-quarters of the time and it doesn't really matter."

"Because he has you as his assistant."

"Do you know what I do, mostly? Sign slips of paper. I okay in Herb's name what other people propose to do."

"What else is administering?"

"Nothing. That's my point."

It was an odd view, in a way, but Tolstoyan too. Napoleon's successes were explained by the fact that his orders were not carried out. But Tolstoy appealed to history whereas Peter said in effect that the sergeants commanded the army. The procedures that unified all the different activities governed the chancellor as well.

"It's not that it isn't a job, Carlotta. The question is, why would anyone want it? Power, you'll say."

"Power."

"Untrue. What power does Herb Laplace have over you?"

"He could fire me."

"Arbitrarily? Not on your life. All he could do is endorse a departmental decision to let you go. And anyone with tenure is out of reach altogether."

"So are you going to withdraw your name?"

"I'm not sure. Bellini probably thinks I already have. Maybe I want to blame it on the Faculty Senate."

"You can go back to teaching."

"Here?"

He might have meant only that there wasn't much of a future for a Classics teacher at Fort Elbow, but Carlotta doubted it.

"Look at Handel."

He smiled. "Yes, I could always become eccentric."

"Or like Rogerson too."

He smiled. "But he's a Catholic."

"So am I."

"Come on."

"It's true."

"I never would have guessed."

She wasn't sure she liked his reaction. Was he insulting the Church or her?

"I meant, you don't go to Mass, do you?"

"Not as much as I should."

"Where do you go?"

"Not the Newman chapel."

It wasn't much fun telling Peter about Father Floeck. You had to be Catholic to appreciate the enormity of it. Since the bad experience at the Newman chapel, Carlotta had been going to a Russian Orthodox church near the old railroad station. The station had been converted into a restaurant and boutiques, but the church was what it had always been.

Of course Peter would be thinking of the times they had slept together—twice, to be exact. It was all so civilized she could cry. He was unfailingly nice to her and he did not presume that once admitted to her bed he had carte blanche. In fact he never alluded to it at all. Carlotta thought she would prefer more passion and aggressiveness. What was it Valerie had said?

"Peter's skin is smoother than mine ever was."

That was catty. There was something fragile, even overly refined about Peter, breeding carried to a fault, but he was also very, very handsome.

"Peter, you'll make a very good chancellor."

"That's like being a good thief."

"You sound like Matt Rogerson."

"I'm quoting him. He would make an entertaining chancellor."

"I don't think he really believes in higher education."

"His problem is that he does."

Carlotta began to think that Peter really did not want to be chancellor. Good news for Valerie, perhaps. As for herself, Carlotta felt let down by the realization.

Maybe she was wrong.

Maybe Peter was just going through a phase.

He took her to the Great Wall of China for dinner, came home with her afterward. It was their third time.

5

Gil Mayhew brought young Porter along when he flew to Columbus to talk with the governor. Even at twelve thousand feet, Ohio looked vulnerable, what they could see of it through streaking, angry clouds. Porter was rigid in his seat, strapped in tightly, hands clamped to the ends of the flimsy chair arms. The Fairchild could accommodate twelve, but they were the only passengers. The pilot wore a crushed cap, wire-rim sunglasses and the sardonic expression of a mercenary between wars. But his grizzled sideburns suggested he had seen his last battle. He had to settle for flying the Fairchild as if it were a World War II fighter. His flight plan seemed to involve heading straight for any troublesome cloud formation in order to ride out the turbulence. The second officer, a kid whose jaw moved in bovine rhythm as he chewed a mouthful of gum, nodded appreciatively as the little plane bucked and rolled through the rough weather.

"Twenty more minutes," Mayhew said, looking at his watch.

Porter nodded but kept staring straight ahead. He might have been waiting for the switch to be thrown.

"You flown one of these before?" he asked Mayhew.

"Yes."

"Then they do make it?"

"Usually."

Such badinage was not what Porter needed to get through this flight. His lips moved, perhaps in prayer, though the glance he shot at Mayhew suggested a curse.

They ran out of clouds then and despite the pilot's best efforts the rest of the flight was smooth. Mayhew closed his eyes and tried to prepare for the meeting ahead. This was a trip Laplace should have made, but he was in Baton Rouge beating his breast. Peter Kessel had come down with the flu, but it wasn't until ten minutes before the flight was called that he'd decided he couldn't go.

In the terminal Peter stood and looked forlornly down at Mayhew, his garment bag dangling from his hand, like an apprehended student. His face was gray and unshaven; he looked like hell.

"I can't go, Gil."

"Go home to bed."

"You can reach me there if you have to. No, I don't mean that. Call me and let me know how things are going?"

Thus it was that with Porter alone Gil Mayhew flew off to

the meeting. Sometime during the next few hours he hoped a decision would be announced and an end put to the nonstop commotion on campus. The faculty needed a focus for their resentment and that was a principal function of the chancellor.

"A lightning rod," Laplace had told him once. "That's what I am. Students, faculty, staff have a complaint, they unload on me. I take the charge and ground it and that's that."

To know Laplace was to understand why he was universally despised. Maybe a new chancellor would give the position an entirely new spin. Gil Mayhew tried to imagine the Fort Elbow campus flourishing, but he gave it up. He would settle for a little peace and quiet.

Last night the Independent Students Association had run a full-page ad in the *Fort Elbow Tribune* endorsing Matthew Rogerson for chancellor. The centerpiece of the ad was a photograph of a beardless Rogerson smiling angelically at whom it might concern. It looked like his graduation photograph.

Bellini was seated in the governor's outer office when they arrived. He got up and motioned Mayhew into a corner of the room.

"Where's Kessel?"

"He came down with the flu."

"Watson wants to make an announcement today."

"*The* announcement?"

The corners of Bellini's mouth dimpled slightly. "Who have I been for?"

"Peter?"

The great blue lids lowered over his eyes, then lifted again.

"Have you talked with him?" asked Mayhew.

"Watson?"

"Peter."

"Sometimes it's best to move things along. There has been too much fritzing around already."

A door opened and a white-haired, pink-skinned man entered, eyes darting about, the look of a man used to being recognized. While Bellini had been speaking to Mayhew, others had been entering the room, men and women bearing notebooks and cameras. Action-cam operators from local television got into position. Watson's smile was in place, but his brows raised when he looked at Bellini.

"Is he here, Senator?"

Bellini went to the governor and whispered in his ear. Watson glanced at Mayhew, as if he had forgotten to bring Peter. But then Mayhew was waved to the governor's side.

He directed his own unpracticed smile above the reporters who formed a half-moon before them. Watson's announcement was brief, as if he felt he had been let down.

"Dr. Peter Kessel will be the new chancellor of the Fort Elbow campus of the University of Ohio. I am delighted to make this announcement in the presence of officers of the university. Dr. Kessel, alas, is temporarily indisposed . . ."

"Like his predecessor?" came a cynical voice from the rear of the room. Watson ignored the question.

"You will be provided with information on the new chancellor."

He shook Bellini's hand firmly, looking at Mayhew as he did. He had apparently decided to let bygones be bygones.

"Thanks for coming down, Mr. Mayhew."

The governor retreated into his office. Bellini was on his way out of the room. Porter was in the hallway outside.

"I want to find a phone and let Peter know before anyone

else does," Mayhew said, looking around. "Why don't we rent a car and drive back?"

The memory of fear clouded Porter's eyes.

"Fine. If you do the driving."

Mayhew let the phone in Peter Kessel's apartment ring twelve times before he hung up and called his office. Enid was surprised to learn that Dr. Kessel was not in Columbus with Mayhew.

"He doesn't answer at home. He has just been named chancellor."

The secretary let out a squeal of joy. Perhaps it *was* an occasion for celebration, Mayhew thought. The search was over at last.

6

Herb Laplace got the news when he changed planes in St. Louis and called his office. Rose seemed to think he would be glad even if she wasn't.

"I suppose he'll want to bring Enid in here."

Laplace mumbled something. Of course his secretary would be affected by this change, but there had been plenty of time for Rose to get used to it.

"It'll be a nice raise for her," Rose said, which was easier to mention than the pay cut she faced. As secretary to the chancellor, she was top scale.

"Did Peter mention me at the press conference?"

"Oh, he wasn't there. I caught a glimpse of Mr. Mayhew but the governor made the announcement with Senator Bellini standing next to him."

"In Columbus?"

"That's right."

"I can't believe Peter wasn't there. What's the point of calling a press conference except to introduce the new man?"

Rose hadn't thought of it. "Would you like me to check on it?"

"Discreetly."

Laplace hung up, smoked a cigarette and looked out the terminal window at the plane that would take him to Cleveland. He knew himself well enough to recognize the little leap of hope Rose's words had elicited. Hope? Did he think Peter's absence from the press conference meant he really had not been appointed? The face of the ex-chancellor—now ex–acting chancellor as well—sagged as he thought of these months since his fall from grace.

He was better off now, financially, than he had ever been. Whenever he totted up the money coming to him from Danto Associates his mouth watered. And it was pleasant enough, lacerating himself before groups of strangers across the land. As for being chancellor, what a break it was to be free of all that crap at last.

He repeated that last thought, actually forming the words silently. *I am glad I am no longer chancellor*. The only trouble was that it was a lie. Alone in the St. Louis airport, he could admit to himself that he would give his left testicle if he could relive the day of Norah Vlach's death. In his imagination he saw himself raise a single glass to her memory and then drive home for dinner with Lillie. A night like any other. The next day, up and at 'em, back to the office and the routine that had defined his life for years.

Instead he had spent that night in jail and the following morning he was conned into resigning. His spirit was so low by then that he had been easy picking for Kessel and Mayhew and Huile. Let everything happen as it had up to that point, if only he had told them all then to go to hell and toughed it out, getting Bellini on the phone and asking when they could talk football, he would still be chancellor today.

Yesterday he had been happy to learn from Danto's office that the New Orleans talk had been canceled and he could be home a day early. He had the rest of the week free. But now the thought of returning to Kessel's triumph and a permanently altered situation was unwelcome. It would be like coming back from the dead.

It helped some to know that Bellini would regret having supported Peter for the job. Maybe he thought that by backing Peter for chancellor he would have his loyalty and could move ahead with plans for football at the Fort Elbow campus. What a crazy idea anyway. It was unrealistic to think they could ever field a team that would put the campus on the map. It was even less realistic to imagine Peter Kessel leading the crusade for that team. Bellini forgot that once Peter had the job, the state senator's clout would immediately diminish rather than increase. Laplace and Bellini had seen eye to eye, that was why Herb had gone along with the idea; if he hadn't wanted to, there wasn't much Bellini could have done about it.

His flight was called and Laplace claimed his aisle seat in back. Not that it mattered. Smoking was not allowed on this flight. For all they knew, every rivet in the aircraft was loose, the motors were all about to fall off, their lives weren't worth a nickel, but no smoking! What the hell was happening to the world? Laplace could actually imagine Prohibition getting a second chance. As if frightened by the possibility, he bought two beers when the flight attendants came around with the cart.

Above the clouds, looking out over the cottony expanse, Laplace decided that the first thing he would do was talk with Kessel about the football team. Had Peter made any promises to Bellini? Even if he had, he should nix the idea of football at Fort Elbow. How many teams could a state support? Oh, he didn't need reasons like that. He would convince Kessel that under his leadership the university could take a giant step forward as an institution of higher learning. Did Peter intend to be the pawn of a nitwit like Bellini?

Waiting in Cleveland for the commuter to Fort Elbow, Laplace had nearly an hour to kill.

His office phone was busy and so was the phone at home. It was that way for fifteen minutes and it was difficult to pretend to be on the phone and ignore the people waiting to use it. Finally, Laplace called Rogerson's office. After all the busy signals it was almost good to hear the bastard's voice.

"What do you think about Kessel, Matt?"

"It's a shame."

"He won't be a bad chancellor."

Silence. "Haven't you heard?"

"Heard what?"

"Where are you, in a massage parlor?"

"I wish I was. I'm in the Cleveland airport. I called Rose from St. Louis and she told me Peter got the job."

"Sure he did. Posthumously."

"What do you mean?"

"When they went to give him the news, they found him dead."

Chapter Six

1

Abe Herman laughed when Sylvia stood in his doorway and said that Peter Kessel was dead. He thought it was a joke, a bad joke, but the way Sylvia stared at him told him otherwise.

"I thought you liked him," she said.

"Are you serious?"

"Didn't you?"

"Is Peter really dead?"

"I am just passing on what I was told. Now I'm sorry I did."

"But he was just named chancellor!"

"Well, they're going to have to name another one." Sylvia's anger was directed at him.

Abe was almost sorrier to hear that than to hear Peter was dead, initially. He still could not believe that a man as young as Peter was dead.

"What did he die of?"

"I don't know. They just found him."

"Where?"

"At home, I guess."

"Do you know where Peter lived?"

Her eyes drifted away. "I could find it."

"Let's go."

The expression on Sylvia's face made it clear she had no desire to see a dead body.

"Maybe we can be of help."

That got to her. She had a car and they hurried out to it. Help whom do what? It was good Sylvia didn't ask him because he sure as hell didn't know. She got the car started and they were on their way when Abe realized why he was angry. It was as though Peter had died just to cause Abe Herman problems.

"Would he have heard of his appointment?"

Sylvia said, "I don't know."

It was now three in the afternoon. The announcement had been made that morning in Columbus. It seemed unlikely that it had come as a surprise to Peter. He must have known about it. He must have accepted the job before they announced it. It was crazy to think that the news had killed him.

"I wonder when he got back?"

"From where?"

"Columbus."

"Look, why ask me these questions? I don't know any more than I've told you."

"I know that. I'm just wondering out loud."

Peter's condominium overlooked an artificial lake shaped like a figure eight. There was an Oriental-looking wooden bridge across the narrow neck joining the two ovals. Ducks drifted on the water. There was an ambulance in front of Peter's place and several squad cars. An officer blocked their way when they started toward the door.

"We're colleagues," Abe said and added in a lower voice, "officers of the Faculty Senate."

The cop didn't know what to make of that. "No visitors," he said, but his tone was not firm.

"Visitors? This woman is his fiancée."

The cop stepped aside and Abe felt Sylvia's fingers dig into his upper arm. "What a stupid thing to say," she said in a low, furious voice. "If you say it again, I will pull your arm off."

"I thought you liked Peter."

He yelped with pain as she pinched his arm. It brought tears to his eyes and that helped when they got to the door. But despite his tears Abe saw Gilbert Mayhew inside and he called out to the university lawyer. That was their open sesame.

Mayhew recognized them but seemed unsure exactly who they were.

"You found the body?"

Mayhew looked at the detective he had been talking to. "I thought you were going to talk to the press."

"This is Professor Sylvia Woods," Abe said sweetly. "I am Professor Abraham Herman. We are a delegation from the Faculty Senate . . ."

"A delegation?"

"We want firsthand information on what happened to our chancellor."

Mayhew put his hand on Abe's arm. "He may have already been dead when the announcement was made."

The other man—a detective named Ennis—left and Mayhew seemed relieved to tell them what had happened.

An ailing Peter Kessel had begged off the trip to Columbus at the last minute. He had actually gone to the airport. Had he known what the point of the trip was?

"*I* hadn't been told, but *he* may have been. Bellini would know."

"What was wrong with him?"

Mayhew shrugged. "He said it was flu."

"You don't die of flu," Abe said.

Mayhew had driven back from Columbus, arriving in Fort

Elbow at one-thirty. He had dropped his young associate off at his downtown office and gone on to Kessel's apartment. If he had been too ill to go to Columbus, he would have been too ill to go to the office. He had found Kessel behind the wheel of his car in the carport next to his building. When he opened the door, Peter tumbled out onto the concrete.

"I brought him inside," Mayhew said, addressing Sylvia. "I can see now why the police don't like that. I didn't think he was dead."

"Was the door of his apartment open?" Abe asked.

"His keys were in his pocket." Mayhew looked around and lowered his voice. "I was thinking of Laplace. I thought we wouldn't want any but the best publicity for *this* chancellor."

Once inside, Mayhew had seen this was death, not sickness.

"I called the police and I'm still here."

Ennis returned and said to Abe, "There's no reason for you to be here."

Sylvia said, "Thanks for letting us speak to Mr. Mayhew."

Ennis was puzzled by her gratitude, as doubtless she meant him to be.

2

Sylvia decided that Carlotta would need company now. Peter's death was a shock to them all but it was far worse for Carlotta. Valerie thought it was a good idea but didn't want to go herself. "You go, Sylvia." Did Valerie fear her position was now equivocal since Peter had been her rival?

Carlotta wore the stunned look of a child confronting the absurdity of death for the first time, but it was memory rather than a first experience that explained her reaction.

"Let's go someplace. I have to get out of here."

Sylvia suggested they just drive around and Carlotta nodded. At that moment she might have agreed to go to the moon.

A light rain began to fall as they drove, and Carlotta seemed to be addressing it as much as Sylvia.

"My parents died within a month of one another. First my mother, then my father. They had been unconscious for half a year from an automobile accident. I used to sit beside their beds, taking turns, trying to remember the last time I had talked with either of them. That should be important, shouldn't it, the last time we talk with someone?

"How could you know?"

"I guess I thought they would live forever, unconscious but alive, people I must visit. Then one day my mother died."

Carlotta spoke with wonder in her voice, as if her mother had done something hitherto unheard of. As if she had betrayed her.

"I have no clear memory of the last time I spoke with Peter."

Sylvia did, as it happened, but she didn't say so. It was pretty obvious Carlotta was talking to herself. Sylvia and Peter had discussed Carlotta.

"What do you think?" Peter had asked, cocking his head to one side and smiling invitingly. Sylvia could easily imagine him as chancellor.

"The Tolstoys were crazy."

"Do you like the course?"

"I haven't missed a meeting. Carlotta keeps us on the edge of our chairs."

In class, Carlotta had talked of Tolstoy's death, his running away from home, away from Sophia, and then falling ill and dying in a country railway station. They would not let Sophia into the room while Leo was still alive. Carlotta had slides for that lecture, and there was a poignant photograph of Sophia being turned away from the door of the little station. In her diary she complained bitterly that she was not permitted to see Leo. It had been Carlotta's point that Tolstoy was not so much running away from his wife as running toward something else. What?

"Innocence. Youth. Escape from the body."

What did such words mean now when Peter lay dead? Carlotta had intimated a lofty significance to the final flight and death of the great Russian author, but she was overwhelmed by a death close to her. Sylvia tried to remember if she had told Peter the subject of that lecture.

Both hands on the wheel, the rain washing over the car and creating a mesmerizing effect on the wet blacktop, lights repeating themselves, Sylvia assured herself that she had not spoken of Tolstoy's death to Peter. It seemed important. Superstitiously, she would have felt that she had brought death to Peter if that had been the topic of their last conversation.

They were near the airport when Carlotta began to snap out of it.

"Do you have any cigarettes?"

"No!"

"I think I would smoke one if I had some."

"Not in my car."

"Just now all the nonsense about health and taking care of yourself rings pretty hollow. Peter was healthy as a horse."

Carlotta sobbed as she said it and then the tears came, thank God, and Sylvia knew it would be better now.

"I might have one with you," she lied.

"Did you ever smoke?"

"Tobacco?"

"I never tried anything else. I don't mean to sound virtuous. People talk about drugs being everywhere, but I never had a chance to say no to them."

Sylvia found herself in the exit lane for the airport, so she followed it. She continued on to short-term parking and when she turned off the windshield wipers and then the engine, the rain sounded drumlike on the roof.

"Want to go inside and have coffee?"

"Okay." But Carlotta didn't sound enthusiastic.

"There's an umbrella in the backseat."

Carlotta sat with her eyes closed, a small smile on her lips. "I love that sound."

"The womb."

Carlotta looked at her. "Do you suppose?"

The sounds of airplanes were sonar probes, asking whether there was life in this metal uterus, reporting back twins. It was half-tempting to sit there and just listen to the rain, but Sylvia reached over the seat for the umbrella and pushed open her door. Rain swept into the car.

She hopped out and opened the umbrella but she was already drenched when she got around to the other door. Carlotta had eased it open and now flung it wide and jumped under the protection of the umbrella. Ten feet away was a covered walkway and soon they were in the vast echoing expanse of the terminal, where amplified announcements warred with one another.

The waiting areas were filled with travelers who looked as if they wished the airplane had never been invented. After buying plastic cups of coffee, Sylvia and Carlotta found seats facing a window that ran with rain and through which the twinkling lights of taxiing planes were impressionistically visible.

"What did he die of?" It was possible to speak as long as they both looked in the same direction.

"He was found dead in his car."

"Suicide?"

Sylvia was shocked. "No. He just died."

"Of what?"

"No one said. I assumed natural causes." Sylvia felt stupid that she did not know. She had assumed Peter had died of heart failure or something. She had no experience with death.

"Causes can be natural without the death being so."

"What do you mean?"

"Was he killed?"

"Carlotta, I don't think so."

"He hadn't been ill." And she repeated an earlier remark. "He was healthy as a horse."

"Had he said something to you?"

"Oh, no."

These were disturbing questions and Sylvia tried to dismiss them. Surely something would have been said by Mayhew or the police if Peter's death had been either suicide or caused by . . . By what? By whom? was the more relevant question, and that made it all silly. Who would want to kill Peter Kessel?

3

Peter Kessel had been poisoned.

Handel received the news from Laura the following morning much as he had news of the fall of Laplace only weeks before. Peter's poisoning, like Peter's death, had yet to sink into the provostal pate and Handel, feeling a surge of emotion within his breast as the magnificent chords of Bach coursed through him, smiled and nodded. Laura came closer and removed the headphones.

"Pe-ter Kes-sel was poi-soned," she said, her mouth forming the words exaggeratedly, her eyes widening and narrowing in harmony with her lips. "Someone killed him."

"Nonsense."

"Frederick! It's on the news. I'm not making it up. He died of arsenic poisoning. The question is, who did it?"

A prior question was how he was to prevent these dreadful events from threatening his peace of mind. Of course, he was sorry about Peter, although he had never found the young man thoroughly congenial. He was learned, he was brilliant, but there was no gainsaying the fact that he had preferred administration to the life of scholarship. Handel felt that he himself had been impressed into the service, the Billy Budd of administration, but Peter had taken the king's shilling willingly. Not only that, he had aspired to advancement. Imagine, thinking of sitting where Herbert Laplace had sat as an advancement. Laplace. Ah, there was the needed buffer.

"Laplace will handle it."

"Laplace," she said with scorn in her voice and scorn on her face. "The police will handle it. This is murder."

He retrieved his headphones and clamped them into place. Think of Bach being played on, unheard. Bach was dead, the musicians on the recording might, some of them, be dead, but still the concerto played on. Music seemed a defense against death. Laura was talking, perhaps to him, her mouth moving, but all he heard was Bach.

There were any number of savage breasts which music could not soothe. Laplace called and Laura would not tell him the provost was on his way to the office despite Handel's pantomimed instructions.

"I'm coming there, Fred. We have to get our ducks in a row before the police talk to us."

"What do you mean?"

"Haven't you heard about Peter?"

"Yes."

"He was poisoned, killed. Someone did it. The police will want to know who. We have to prevent them from connecting his death to the college. To the work of the search committee."

Handel acquiesced in Laplace's coming. At least it was a legitimate excuse for not going to the office. Laura went into a tizzy.

"Here? Why here? It's not yet nine o'clock in the morning."

She circled the room as she said this and then disappeared as if by centrifugal force down the hall whence the sounds of her ablutions soon emanated. Reluctantly, Handel put away his earphones and turned off his CD player. His eyes drifted to his bookshelves. Dear God, if only he could once more lead the life of the mind. He would resign as provost, he would. Study and teaching, a little more writing, that was what he wanted. He would be content with that until his own death came and when he taught or wrote on the mystics, he would try to do so as one of them. He would purge his soul of unworthy desires, aspire only to the eternal.

The eternal. It was an odd thought that whatever that term referred to, Peter Kessel was there now. A disturbing realization. Handel felt the prick of skepticism, his equivalent of the Pauline thorn. How could he believe in something so impossibly good as eternal bliss? No matter. He would live as if he believed, making the Pascalian wager.

What had begun as a quasi-prayer degenerated into an all-too-typical probing of the Handel navel. How shallow he was, how trivial. *Miserere mei, Domine.*

Laplace slipped past the door when Laura opened it and pushed it closed himself. He looked at them over his shoulder.

"I don't think I was followed."

"What have you done?" Laura asked. She had stepped back as if to give him a second chance to notice the outfit she was wearing: a gray pleated skirt, a black vest intricately embroidered, a pink blouse that made her hair more silvery.

Laplace looked disappointed. "Didn't you tell her?"

What an odd thought, keeping secrets from Laura. He had of course repeated to Laura Laplace's strange remarks about the police.

He said now, "Since we know nothing, it would be a very short conversation, Herb."

"It will take a while to convince them you know nothing."

Laura, deciding she had changed in vain, led the way onto the sun porch where forty-seven potted plants sat, hung or stood, all of them relentlessly growing.

"That's donkey's tail," Laura said, as Laplace stared openmouthed at a hanging pot. The acting chancellor spun and looked at her as if it had been an insult.

Laura went for coffee and Handel assumed an attentive expression and sighted on a great blade of mother-in-law's tongue that seemed about to get intimate with Laplace's ear.

"The thing to stress is that we knew nothing of Peter's private life."

"I didn't."

"That's what I'm saying. Who knows what crowd he ran with off campus? Deflect them, that's the idea. We can't have the police making a nuisance of themselves on campus."

It seemed a simple enough plan, provided Peter had had a private life.

"Wasn't he great friends with Carlotta?"

"Don't even say it."

"Why on earth not?"

Laplace tried to be patient with him, and with Laura too when she had poured the coffee and sat with them.

"Herbert, Peter was one of us. He was your assistant. It's silly to think that can be kept a secret. Who do you think poisoned Peter?"

"That's the police's job. My job is to safeguard the reputation of the Fort Elbow campus."

Handel looked at Laura. This was the man whose scandalous behavior had been all but national news, whose resignation had plunged the school into a crisis which had led to the aggravation of the search committee, and he had the gall to suggest that his concern was the reputation of the school.

"I'm sure you'll do your best," Laura said sweetly.

"I'm meeting Mayhew downtown."

They rose, taking this as a signal he was leaving. Laplace, still holding his cup, looked up at them. He put it down and got to his feet.

At the door, he turned to Handel. "While I'm incommunicado, you of course are the highest available spokesman for the university."

Handel protested, on the verge of saying that was Peter Kessel's job, and then fell back. Laura's hand cupped his elbow. Laplace, about to say something more, decided against it. He slipped out the door and went at a half-trot up the street to where he had parked his car.

"What a silly little man," Laura said.

But it was a judgment she would have pronounced on any male she had yet met.

4

For some years, death had made Rogerson sheepish, almost embarrassed. Who was he to still be around at sixty-two while kids were dropping like flies? He had outlived most of his heroes by many years, which was bad enough, but mourning someone the age of Peter Kessel made him feel like an intruder among the living. And to have the news come from Sylvia.

Rogerson lived alone in the four-bedroom house in which he had raised his family, more or less. When they bought it they had wanted size but it no longer seemed large to him. He could not imagine living in a smaller house, let alone an apartment. He rotated among the bedrooms. Well, not quite. He avoided the room he had shared with Marge. The bed was a battleground on which he had suffered too many defeats. Marge's hysterectomy should have turned her into a mink, but she might have taken a vow. He did not want to talk of the marriage debt, what was owed him. All he wanted was to make love to his wife. Sex as forgiveness.

"I've been driving around in the rain with Carlotta," Sylvia said without preamble when Rogerson picked up the phone.

"Is it raining?"

"Are you drinking?"

"Come over and I will."

"That's why I called. I think Carlotta will be all right."

It was Rogerson's experience that unintelligible conversations had a way of becoming intelligible by themselves, but Sylvia's obscure remark was followed by others.

"Has anyone questioned you about Peter?"

"What the hell for?"

"You heard it was poison, didn't you?"

"It?"

The cause of Peter's death. My God. No point in expressing his shock over the phone. He told her to come quickly.

When he heard her car in the driveway he opened the

door so she could dash in from the rain. Somewhat to his surprise, she ran into his arms. What a plush, comfortable thing the female body was. She told him what she knew about Peter after he extricated himself, took her hand and led her into the kitchen, where he poured them each a drink.

"I've talked about this with Herman and Valerie and Carlotta and now you, and I still can't believe it."

"Death comes like a thief in the night."

"Peter died this morning."

It was that kind of conversation, more therapy than sensible, and he let her go on. His problem was different: death, disaster and other tragedies no longer surprised him. The intervals separating them had come to seem unnatural.

In the living room she picked up the book he had put down to answer the door.

"Max Brand?"

"His real name was Faust."

"You're kidding."

"Scout's honor." He retrieved his book. *Blood on the Trail*. "He's not a great writer, just a reputable hack, but I enjoy him."

"The American genre?" Sylvia asked.

Rogerson did not have a theory up his sleeve. He liked Zane Grey and Max Brand and that was that. As entertainment.

"Someone should write about the hack writer. I don't consider the appellation negative. Dr. Johnson wrote to order as did many others. Think of the *Life of Savage*. The hack writer himself is reponsible for the unfavorable estimate of his kind."

This was dangerously like a theory, but Rogerson was still thinking of Brand who turned out fiction all morning and then wrote awful epics with a quill pen in the afternoon.

"He didn't realize that it was in the morning that he produced literature."

"Literature?"

"Literature is anything you'll read twice."

They progressed to the study, where Sylvia did not sit but looked at his shelves. Humming, she studied the spines of books, drew out a volume and paged through it. She put it back and repeated the action several times.

"What a crazy collection."

"Feel free."

Their eyes met, her face trembled and she burst into tears. Holding her was dangerous but he really had no choice. He could stand loneliness if there was nothing to contrast it with. He and Sylvia were old friends, usually their get-togethers were just food and drink and talk, but this was different. Soothing a weeping female is what we pray Our Father not to be led into.

She calmed down, stepped back, took out a Kleenex. "Everyone seems determined to keep Peter's death unconnected with the campus."

"Who's everyone?"

"Abe. Valerie. Laplace."

"Why?"

She looked at him. "Isn't that best?"

"For whom? If he was killed, there's a killer."

"Who do you think did it?"

"God knows. I thought arsenic was hard to get."

"Can you imagine someone actually poisoning him?"

The question made Valerie's face pop before Rogerson's mind. "There are his competitors for the chancellor's job."

"That includes you."

"Can I freshen your drink?" he asked, wagging his eyebrows.

"It's no joke. Peter is dead. Murdered."

She was right, of course. It was no joke.

5

Bellini was furious and profane, so angry Mayhew could not stop the thought that the senator sounded guilty rather than concerned. Mayhew shook his head, and glared at the phone. His mind was turning to jelly. Peter had been Bellini's candidate, he had bulled through the appointment yesterday morning, overcoming the reluctance of the governor as well as of Peter himself.

"It's in the hands of the police now," Mayhew said. He had felt like anything but an officer of the court in Kessel's apartment, aware that the police regarded what he had done and what he said as suspicious. He didn't blame them.

It was hard now to know what he was thinking of when he had eased Peter up from the concrete and carried him into the house, having unlocked and propped open the door beforehand. The key had been on the same ring as the ignition key. But it had not crossed his mind that Peter was dead. Peter was what? Thirty years old, slightly more. So what if he had been feeling ill that morning?

But later, speaking to the police, Mayhew felt like an idiot. The truth was he had been carrying a corpse around, the corpse of someone who, it turned out, had been poisoned. That meant he had been mucking around on the scene of the crime.

"I don't think he was poisoned in his car," he retorted.

"You don't, huh?"

"Look, this morning he was supposed to fly to Columbus

with me. He felt sick and decided not to come. He must have been already poisoned."

"That's what you think, huh?"

The retort that occurred to him was, "Stick it in your ear," but he didn't use it.

"To hell with the police," Bellini said over the phone. "Come up here and tell them."

A pause. "I'm in Fort Elbow. In my office. Laplace is with me. Do you think you can get here without being followed?"

"Followed?"

"I want a secret meeting."

"When?"

"Can you come now?"

"I'll be there."

"Be careful."

It was kid stuff to think he would be followed. Wasn't it? He left his office by the back door and went down the stairs all the way to the basement, the backs of his legs almost cramping from the unusual exercise. His car was in the basement garage, but he went on foot the six blocks to the courthouse where Bellini had his senatorial office. An unshaven Laplace sat in a studded leather chair, a glass in his hand. Mayhew hoped it was water. Herb looked uncomfortably like he had after his episode with the police. Mayhew's unease increased when Bellini revealed the point of the meeting.

"I've been on the phone to Governor Watson. He agrees we can't prolong this goddam search. But he wants assurance Herb will be accepted."

"Herb?"

"To succeed himself. Peter was never inaugurated. He's no John Paul I."

"Do you want to be chancellor again?" Mayhew asked Herb.

Laplace lowered his head and regarded Gil through his brows. "You sound incredulous."

"I am."

"Well, get over it," Bellini said. "I want you to pass the word and get everyone in line."

"Damn it, Herb, if you hadn't resigned, none of this would have happened."

"You talked me into it, Gil."

Mayhew looked at Bellini. "That's right, I did. At your insistence, Bellini. Well, this time, you can do it without me. This is a farce."

"Sit down," Bellini said in a soft voice. "I don't blame you for being mad. I'm mad too. None of this should have happened. But the basic fault was Herb's, out racing the cops while he's drunk as a skunk. If he'd kept his nose clean, we would have been all right. Who knows what this will do to the athletic program?"

For Bellini, that was a speech. He was single-minded, you had to give him that. Throughout these crazy weeks, the one thing he had kept his sights on was football at the Fort Elbow campus. Everything else was secondary, Herb, Peter. And me, Mayhew recognized. He wished now he had walked out rather than sat down. It occurred to him that he was a weak man, and the realization was an epiphany. A surprise, but also something he had somehow already known. Bellini knew it. Even Laplace knew it.

"I wonder who killed Peter Kessel?"

"That we'll leave to the police," Bellini said.

"You found him, Gil?" Laplace asked.

"Yeah."

He had gone to tell him he was the next chancellor and here he was a day later being enlisted to put Herb Laplace back in the job. Why the hell not? Who else was there?

"The senate will object, but then they would have objected to Peter as well."

"The senate." Herb spoke the word as if he were just learning it. "What an assembly of idiots."

"Watch it, Herb," Bellini said. "You want their support."

"Gill will take care of that."

"What about your career as a lecturer?"

"I'm a born educator, gentlemen. The lecture circuit was a poor substitute for the real thing. I belong in the university."

It was difficult to disagree.

PART THREE

A Darkling Plain

Chapter Seven

1

As soon as Peter Kessel's body was released by the police, it was cremated and readied for shipment to his sister in Maine. Abe Herman approved of the promptness. Christians had the unsettling habit of prolonging the obsequies for the deceased. And indeed they did not in this case forego their habits completely. The senate voted that a memorial ceremony should be held in the crematorium, so there they all were in what looked like a set from *Star Trek* listening to Herb Laplace eulogize his dead assistant.

Abe closed his eyes and tried to think of nothing, always a difficult task, but almost impossible with the drone of Laplace's voice. Was this the man who allegedly was cleaning up on the lecture circuit? In extenuation, it would be difficult to speak over the remains of a man whose death was due to poison when the identity of the poisoner was still unknown. Was it someone in this room?

Abe's eyes snapped open. He had never thought of that before but of course it would be the first thing that would occur to the police. Newly named chancellor poisoned. Why? To prevent him from taking office, what else? And who among them had been dismayed to learn of Peter's appointment?

Abe Herman, for one. His own candidacy might be little more than a token one in the eyes of others, but in his heart of hearts he wanted the job. For one thing, he knew he could do at least as good a job as anyone else in the running. The sight of Matt Rogerson was irksome. It was difficult to tell what the old bastard thought of his student supporters, one of whom was in Abe's logic course.

"So she told me," Rogerson had said when Abe mentioned it. "What text do you use?"

"My own."

"I don't know it."

"It was privately printed."

Actually, the book had been one of his better entrepreneurial ideas. He had set the text on the desktop publishing software in the registrar's office, had it printed at InstyPrint and ring-bound. He had a thousand printed the first time; there was nothing to be gained from a longer run at such a printer, and his unit cost was $1.14. He sold them for $19.95 to his students, bypassing the bookstore and the middleman. Two more semesters of the course and he would have sold out, a tidy profit.

"I'd like to see a copy."

"I'll give you one."

It was a good book, Abe had no doubt of that, but one more presentation of the propositional calculus was unlikely to interest Rogerson.

Laplace was gripping the lectern with both hands, a bad sign. He had the look of a man in search of a thread for what he was saying. This could go on a very long time. Gilbert Mayhew seemed to be hanging on Herb's words. Abe had had an unusually cordial conversation with the lawyer just outside.

"We have to speed up the process, Abe."

"How so?"

"How long has it been since the search committee was set up?"

How long is it from mid-September to early November? "It's an important decision."

"I agree. And ordinarily we could afford to go about it at our leisure. Peter's death changes that."

Mayhew professed to be worried that the murder of Peter Kessel would bring undesirable publicity to the university and suggested it would be a far better situation with a new chancellor installed.

"Do you have a new candidate?"

"Let's talk about it."

And he squeezed Abe's arm. Was it possible that the arrow would now point to him?

This was a pleasant thought, far more pleasant than listening to Laplace or trying to think of nothing. Ataraxy. Kessel had used the word more than once. If you hope for nothing you cannot be disappointed. That was what he was trying to do by trying to think of nothing, but it didn't work. So daydream about Abraham Herman, chancellor.

Such fantasy made it clear what a pain in the ass the senate must be to the administration. Abe would not want someone like himself keeping up a steady drumbeat of criticism, putting forward an alternative agenda for the institution, picking, picking, picking. But all that had obviously captured the attention of Mayhew. The lawyer knew no move could be made without consulting with Abe Herman, so why not put him in the driver's seat and let him run the place straight out?

Silence fell. Apparently Laplace was through. He stood

now with bowed head. Abe stirred uncomfortably in his chair. This was hard duty for an agnostic. Herb hesitated, then made a forty-five–degree turn, and bowed at the bronze urn containing Peter's ashes. Everyone followed suit and Abe had no choice, but he felt like an idiot bobbing his head at the urn.

Outside, Valerie Kraft came up to him and laid a glove on his arm.

"Did Mayhew speak to you?"

"What about?"

"They're up to something."

"He said he thought we ought to speed things up."

"We?"

"The process."

"Abe, do you think they think we're part of the process? Don't be ridiculous. Who do they plan to ram down our throats this time?"

"Didn't Mayhew tell you?"

She gave him a steely look. "I refused to discuss the matter with him."

"Good for you."

"Are you in it with them, Abe?"

Maybe if he hadn't been daydreaming in the chapel about Mayhew and company naming him chancellor he would have made a more plausible denial. But in his heart he had already signed on with the establishment, so long as he was their candidate. Valerie's face hardened into contempt and she strode away.

2

When she left Abe, Valerie asked Carlotta and Sylvia to have coffee with her, something very important had come up. Carlotta's eyes were red from the emotions of the ceremony, but Sylvia seemed eager to get away from the crematorium. "What a word. I'm surprised the dairy industry hasn't objected."

Carlotta came with Valerie, but Sylvia had her own car, so they agreed to meet at Wang Too's near the campus. The suggestion was Sylvia's. It seemed an odd place for coffee but no doubt Sylvia wanted lunch.

"I still can't believe it," Carlotta said when they were under way.

Valerie sighed in lieu of an answer. She never knew what to reply to such remarks.

"He would have made a good chancellor, Val."

"We'll never know now."

She wanted to save what she had to say until the restaurant.

Sylvia was hungry, no doubt of that. She had won ton soup, two egg rolls and enough shrimp fried rice to feed them all. Carlotta wanted only an egg roll and Valerie ordered chop suey and wished she hadn't. There was an unlimited supply of tasteless tea but Sylvia drank beer with her meal.

"They are already up to something," Valerie said finally. She waited but neither of the other two women picked up on the tone of her voice. "Gil Mayhew, Bellini's henchman, is already maneuvering to fill the chancellorship."

Carlotta waved at air. "Oh, I am so tired of that subject."

"I understand that. I suppose that is what they are counting on, that we will all be so dispirited by Peter's death we will let them do whatever they want."

"What do they want to do?" Sylvia asked.

"Ignore the search committee, mainly. And Abe Herman is in it with them."

Carlotta turned and looked skeptically at Valerie. "What I want to know is who killed Peter."

"It's what they want to sweep under the rug," Valerie said, and it was the start of really getting Carlotta involved.

Was Sylvia with her? That she wasn't against her was better than nothing, but Valerie would have liked more solidarity. There was no way in the world a woman candidate for chancellor would be taken seriously if she didn't fight for it. She told them her plan of attack.

A press conference. She intended to call a press conference, where she would lambaste the sexist bureaucracy and announce her own candidacy. She called Caroline Swift from the restaurant. She knew she could count on Caroline.

Caroline Swift wrote for the *Fort Elbow Tribune*. At forty-five, she was the dean of women journalists in the area and had a good network. Thus far, she had not seen anything in the chancellor search of much interest, but Peter's murder and now the charge that the men were getting together to settle the matter again before Peter was three days dead got her interest.

At three o'clock, they were all set up in the Faculty Lounge, both local television stations, radio, the press, including the student paper. And, by God, Valerie Kraft was ready.

The session in the restaurant had helped her formulate her thoughts, so that when she sat down at her word processor the thing all but wrote itself. The tone was one of the aggrieved victim, but not whining. She spoke with the authority of justice. A small group of men had sat down and picked the next chancellor of the university and had managed to enlist the governor in their petty plan. The beneficiary of their plotting, Peter Kessel, a worthy man, had died within hours of the announcement.

"This tragedy should not blind us to the unfairness of the procedures that led to his nomination. Had Peter Kessel himself come to see this?"

A nice touch. The suggestion had been Caroline's. Keep alive the possibility that the arsenic that killed Peter had been self-applied; in the absence of any other explanation, it had plausibility. But Valerie avoided looking at Sylvia and Carlotta when she said the words.

The questions focused on Valerie's own qualifications for the office of chancellor.

"I think I could do a good job. My main concern is the good of the university. It is the reason for making this statement today. Of course I think it is high time a woman was named to a post at this level."

"Then you are claiming prejudice?"

"I think the facts speak for themselves."

"Are there other candidates?"

"None whose credentials are stronger than mine. I have been associate provost for some time, devoting myself to administrative work. I feel that I have been trained for this job."

"Who are the other candidates?"

"Abraham Herman, president of the Faculty Senate, visibly wants the job. Black Studies has a dark-horse candidate and the union is backing someone. All males."

"You didn't mention Professor Rogerson." This was the

girl from the student paper, what was her name? Amanda Davis.

"Matt Rogerson, that's right. I wouldn't describe him as a serious candidate."

"Why not?" Amanda asked.

"I don't think he considers himself a serious candidate."

"What about the former chancellor?" Caroline broke in. "The womanizer?"

"Herbert Laplace?"

"He's acting chancellor, isn't he?"

"He always was."

The laugh got her off that.

They applauded when it was over and Valerie felt triumphant. Her only regret was that she hadn't done this at the start, but maybe things had to develop the way they had before it was truly effective.

"I'll buy you a drink," she said to Caroline.

"Payola?" But she winked when she said it. "No, thanks. I want to get downtown and write this up."

"How'd I do?"

"Let me put it this way. I don't remember the last time anyone was applauded at a press conference."

3

First had come Mayhew, then Herman, and afterward Handel wanted to hide. He went to the library and holed himself up in the carrel he kept on the second floor, in the medieval section. His microfilm reader was in his office, but his office was no place to be now.

He shut himself in, locked the door and taped sheets of

paper over the narrow window in the door. If it came to that, he would turn off the light to keep his presence here a secret, but he laid his jacket along the bottom of the door to keep the light in and felt that he was safe.

Read? Study? He could weep at how remote such activity seemed. That was his life, to lose himself in the columned folios of centuries-old texts, and for too long, because he had acquiesced in Laura's ambition, he had been prevented from devoting himself full time to what was his reason for being. After Valerie became his assistant, things had been better, much better. He had the best of both worlds, or at least was not wholly cut off from the best world. But everything changed when Herb Laplace was arrested for driving while drunk.

It was, of course, incredibly self-centered to see Laplace's humiliation and the turmoil within the university since, even the death of Peter Kessel, as a nuisance to himself—but, God forgive him, that is how he did feel about it all. He longed to leave this contentious, conniving, petty world and be alone with himself, his books. His God? Yes, that too. Handel dreamed of the spiritual life as other men dream of women, but now, alone in his carrel, cowering, craven, a weakling, he saw his yearning for the divine as a delusion, a kind of self-deception that trivialized what it purported to exalt.

If he were serious, his course was clear. Resign as provost. Silence Laura once and for all. Root out from himself the weed of ambition that had made him amenable to Laura's nagging. Take early retirement and devote himself not to reading about, writing about or forming learned opinions about the interior life, but to the interior life itself. Prayer. Fasting. His mouth watered at the prospect, but he recognized that this was merely the reverse of his desire not to be importuned by Gilbert Mayhew and Abe Herman.

"I have to ask you one question before I go on," Mayhew had said. After the ceremony for poor Peter, the lawyer had separated Handel from Laura and taken him to his law office downtown.

"Yes?" Although the building was new, the offices of Mayhew's firm suggested the twenties or earlier. There was wainscoting on the walls, much brass and rippled glass, all overdone, but it had an imposing effect.

"Do you want to be the next chancellor?"

"My God, no!"

"Good. Good." Mayhew held out his palm like a traffic cop. "It was a pro forma question, but I could not go on as I will if you yourself had aspirations."

"I don't."

"Very well. Whom would you prefer as chancellor?"

"Mr. Mayhew, I wish none of this had arisen. Who would have thought a few months ago that we would be caught up in discussions of this kind?"

"You are referring to the time when Herb Laplace was chancellor."

"Yes."

"It was more peaceful then, wasn't it?"

"If only he had behaved himself."

"We could go back to that time, Professor. We could ask Herb to take the job again."

"He is still doing it anyway."

"That's right."

"Do you think he will be named?"

"If certain things happen."

He might have known the solution could not be that simple.

"It is important that Herb be welcomed back. He will be named if it is clear that he is the choice of the faculty."

"He has made enemies, you know."

"You are not among them, I hope."

"No, no. I told you. I look back on his time as chancellor as a happy time."

"Then help him regain the post. I want you to enlist support for him."

He was caught between the enormously attractive prospect of the return of the status quo ante and the repellent suggestion that he in effect campaign for Herb among the faculty.

"My assistant is a candidate, too."

"Valerie Kraft."

"Yes."

"She has no chance of becoming chancellor."

"She thinks she does."

"Is she your candidate?"

Supporting her in the abstract had been easy, but the thought of Valerie sitting in the chancellor's office surprised a chauvinist streak in Handel. Valerie was one thing as his assistant, but as his superior, she might turn out to be uncomfortably like Laura. In any case, it was Laplace he wanted. He wanted everything to be again exactly as it had been before.

He promised Mr. Mayhew to do all he could to develop support for Herb's return as chancellor. It was the only way to escape. He was so eager to go, he turned down the offer of a ride to campus with a junior partner as chauffeur and rode the bus, his ears assaulted for forty minutes by a portable radio played at an unbelievable volume. He sat as far away from this sonar violence as he could, but it would have been necessary to leave the state to get out of range. Finally, a mile from campus, he got off and walked the rest of the way. The unwonted exercise made him sore and testy, not the best condition in which to meet Abe Herman, who seemed to have been lurking about, awaiting his return.

"Handel, we have to strike while the iron is hot. I think I can get the senate in line. What I need to know is, do I have your support?"

"You are doing a fine job in the senate."

Abe had one hand clamped on his head as if he were holding it on. He closed his eyes. "I want your support as chancellor."

"As chancellor? My dear fellow, I am the provost . . ."

"I want to be chancellor," Herman said through gritted teeth, glancing at Basil who was hunched over an open file drawer but as usual attending to every word spoken. Herman took Handel's elbow and steered him into the inner office.

"Is Valerie here?" Handel called to Basil as he was propelled away.

"Haven't seen her," Basil trilled.

Herman shut the door after them. "Fred, I shouldn't have begun that way. I'm sorry. But the situation is urgent. I repeat. I am a candidate for chancellor. Rather important support has come my way. This morning I spoke with Mayhew, the university counsel. He gave me to understand that he will back my candidacy."

"He told you that!"

Herman had taken understandable umbrage at his incredulous tone. He took his hand from his head and rubbed his chin. He visibly got control of himself.

"I, too, was surprised. Perhaps more pleased than you seem to be."

"It was surprise I expressed, nothing more."

"With Mayhew and Bellini in my corner, I plan to make a move. I want to force a choice in the senate and I need every vote I can get."

It was the sort of problem Valerie handled, but obviously he couldn't enlist her help now. He did a despicable thing.

"I will do everything I can," he said to Herman.

"All I want is your vote."

"Then rest assured."

Having committed himself to two incompatible courses of action, Handel fled his office, seeking refuge in the faculty office building. He had the absurd notion that he would find sanctuary with Matthew Rogerson.

"I liked your article in *Speculum* on the beguinage in Ghent," Matt said. On any other occasion he would have been flattered and delighted, but now it scarcely registered. "I saw Migne's *Latin Patrology* in the catalogue of a Minnesota dealer. Twenty dollars a volume."

"A bargain!"

"That's what I think."

There was the momentary delusion that he had indeed escaped the agony of his conflicting promises, but Rogerson turned the conversation to Peter Kessel.

"Was there some kind of tension between Peter and Valerie?"

"Tension? What tension?"

"Actually," Rogerson said, "my money is on Mrs. Laplace. She probably laced Peter's coffee with arsenic because he was constantly harassing her husband."

Handel was simply not in the mood for such banter, not after his inglorious talks with Mayhew and Herman. He lied that he was expected elsewhere and fled.

So now he sat in his carrel, his face in his hands, unable

even to weep over the oppressive circumstances of his existence. Resign? If there was any justice, he would be fired. Like a child, he thought of feigning illness as the only escape from the mess he had gotten himself into.

Just thinking of feeling ill made him feel ill. Where was the pain? His head? His stomach? His feet? The pain transferred to the location of which he thought. He decided it was in his stomach. An ulcer? Poison?

My God! Whoever had poisoned Peter Kessel had poisoned him as well. He clutched his stomach. There was no doubt it was the location of his pain. But then he thought of Laura and the location shifted. Where he felt pain now was definitely in his neck.

4

Amanda Davis had talked with Rogerson about majoring in Philosophy and had been difficult to dissuade. She had almost enough credits to graduate in chemistry and a switch now would prolong her stay on campus.

"I'm in no hurry."

"Well, of course, if you're independently wealthy."

He had meant it as a joke. But for her, in the phrase, money was no object. Her mother had been enriched by the insurance company when her father sickened and died while working in the lab of what Amanda delicately called a major company.

"What does your mother do?"

The girl began to speak, then stopped. Well, what child is not ashamed of its parent? He did not press her. Old widowers had to be careful where enriched widows are concerned, lest their motives be suspected. If Mama was as meatless as Amanda she was safe from the concupiscence of Matthew Rogerson. Still, he liked the way the girl's lower lip came out when she puffed and made her bangs rise and fall. This was a paragraph ending rather than a period. Sentences ended with a drop of her head which had the effect of tucking her chin into her flat chest. The question about her mother brought on a sort of ellipsis. Her hunted animal's eyes stared at him through her bangs.

"I want to devote the rest of my life to philosophy."

"What brought this on?"

"You."

She had been sitting in on his class where of late he had been digressing on Abelard, in particular on the last days of the gelded lily, spent at Cluny where he died in a way that edified the monastic community. All's well that ends well had been more or less his theme.

"Life draws to an end in either of two ways, as tragedy or as farce."

That was his thesis and though his examples were all distantly historical his memory delivered up his private necrology as he spoke. All his dead streamed over the bridge. He had not thought death had undone so many, but the ghostly crowd continued to grow. It was difficult not to think of Peter Kessel most of all. In any case, in a back row of the class, slack jawed, listening only, not taking notes, sat Amanda Davis.

Rogerson was in the library stacks, paging through Maine de Biran and contemplating this strange young woman when Abe Herman found him. The bald logician stood at the end of the aisle, hands on opposite eye-high shelves, as if for support, and stared at Rogerson.

"Valerie has just held a press conference!"

"It's about time."

"Matt, I'm serious. She dumped all over us."

It was not too much to say that Abe Herman was upset. For purposes of this report, Valerie Kraft had become The Bitch.

"She is playing the feminist card, Matt. Everything to this point has been a male chauvinist plot to deny her what she manifestly deserves, to lord or lady it over us all."

"You don't want her as chancellor?"

The question was a touch of the whip. "You're kidding. You've seen what she's done as provost."

"Handel is provost."

"Ha!"

"You want to be chancellor."

Abe's eyes closed and shut. He spoke with soft vehemence. "Yes."

"You poor devil."

"Don't, Matt, for God's sake. This is serious. This is our future. Don't think I haven't got support." He paused and then seemed to decide to throw caution to the winds. "Mayhew and Bellini are behind me. Handel himself is in my corner."

There was the sound of a sob. Abe turned his great cabbage leaf of an ear and waited. Crying. There was no doubt of it. Someone was crying, and nearby. Abe was clearly not glad to think that he had been overheard. He began to search the stacks for the lachrymose intruder. Rogerson stayed where he was. The prospect of finding some disconsolate student, undone by the duties of this make-believe world, did not appeal. But the crying was not in the stacks.

Rogerson moved toward a closed carrel door and put his

ear against it. There was no doubt that the sobbing came from there. He stepped back and tilted his head so he could read the number, but even as he did so he realized this was Handel's hideaway. He tapped on the door with two knuckles.

The crying ceased. Abe was back, breathing noisily at Rogerson's side. He grabbed the knob and began to rattle it.

"It's Handel," Rogerson whispered to Abe, but this had the effect of lending new vigor to Abe's twisting of the handle. He began pounding on the door with the flat of his free hand.

"Come out of there, Handel."

"Library silence will be observed in the stacks at all times," Rogerson quoted with relish.

There was the sound of the door being unlocked. It opened. Handel blinked out at them, his eyes streaming tears. Abe Herman was not reassured by the condition of his supporter, but he insisted on telling the provost the details of Valerie's press conference. Rogerson suggested they talk in the carrel. He shut the door on the two of them and hurried between the stacks. Amanda was waiting for him. How infinitely preferable to a colleague she seemed.

5

Bellini called from Columbus, which is how Mayhew first heard the news.

"We got another one."

"What do you mean?"

"Valerie Kraft's been poisoned."

He heard it before Bellini said it, or so it seemed. As if her death were the logical conclusion of something, to be expected, inevitable. The press conference. He would not have said it aloud, but that seemed the premise of which Valerie's death was the conclusion.

He turned on the television, without the sound, and flicked through the channels, but the only news was cable. It was on that screen that he had watched the local news just hours before and listened to Valerie's self-serving interpretation of what was going on. Bellini was still talking.

"Get in touch with Laplace. I want to meet with him first thing in the morning. This thing has really gotten out of hand. Have Huile there too."

He told Bellini that he would set up the morning meeting and after he had hung up he turned off the television. Valerie Kraft dead.

Peter Kessel. Now Valerie. Anyone who didn't see a connection with the search for a new chancellor was crazy. It was possible to imagine Valerie doing away with Peter and vice versa, but who would want to kill them both? He picked up the phone, consulted the university directory, and dialed.

"Who's next?" Abe Herman asked after Mayhew identified himself.

"Maybe you. I called to see how you are."

"You have the details?"

"I just learned."

"She was found in her office, dead at her desk."

"Found by whom?"

"Sylvia Woods."

Sylvia had been working in her office and saw the light on in the provost's office when she was on her way out to her car. She had thought the vice-provost had fallen asleep. There was a carton of fruit juice on the desk.

"Sylvia told you all this?" asked Mayhew.

"She's here now. They questioned her for hours."

"She should have called me."

"Maybe you should come now."

Herman lived nearby. He had the top floor of a huge gingerbread mansion that had been renovated and saved from ruin by one of the band of zealots whose religion was the recent past of the city. It stood in a square mile of monuments to the affluence of a century ago, the architecture of ostentation favored by the machinists turned farm-implement manufacturer, automaker, miller, food broker. Here they had dwelt in their high, proud houses among moneylenders and printers and, say it, lawyers. At night the eye was spared the pinks and blues and soft grays the restorers had painted them.

Mayhew got out of his car, locked it and, as he was starting toward the house, stopped. Two puffing joggers plodded past in the night, Ponce de Leóns, determined to breast the tape of eternal youth. Weird. The house loomed over him as he approached it, its top floor alight like a stand of birthday candles.

It was not unlike arriving at a party late. Abe in shirt sleeves, the hair on the sides of his head wild, a glass in hand, opened the door to him and stood aside with an elaborate bow that did not suggest complete sobriety. Gil was inside before he saw Josephine Findley, an elbow on the mantel, holding forth to the two women sitting on the corduroy couch. None of the women looked at him, until Abe had closed the door noisily.

The blonde was Sylvia Woods and the woman seated next to her was Caroline Swift of the *Tribune*. Josephine, of course, was the scourge of the local bar, her reputation made when she successfully brought suit against the Ice-Fishers Club for excluding women. This semiserious club took its name from the men who fished the frozen surface of the river on the rare occasions when it did freeze. Their clubhouse was downtown and Josephine's argument had been that important business was done there over lunch from which women were excluded. In these parlous times, it seemed pointless to appeal. Josephine and her clients had then applied for membership, but the decision had been delayed for nine months because the decision had not mandated increasing the membership and there was a list of approved candidates waiting for death to create an opening among the select seventy-two. Seventy-two was the number of Our Lord's disciples, presumably fishermen all, if not through ice.

"Are you representing the university?" Josephine asked Mayhew.

"I am university counsel."

Josephine turned to Sylvia. "Be careful."

Abe said, "I invited Mayhew here, Josephine. This is my apartment."

Josephine occupied the first floor of the house, it emerged, and had been having an after-dinner drink with Caroline when they heard the news. Sylvia's arrival had drawn their attention and they had come up.

"Coming immediately after Valerie's magnificent news conference," Josephine said, "this suggests a pattern that must not be permitted to develop."

"This" turned out to be the prolonged questioning to which Sylvia had been subjected by the police rather than the death of Valerie.

Not only had Sylvia lunched with Valerie, she had been at the press conference, had stopped at the provost's office to see if Valerie wanted to go out for dinner—she didn't; she was still too high from the triumph with the media—and later had been the one to discover the body. It was not surprising that the police had felt she knew things they should know.

"She must have gone to one of the vending machines off the lobby of the main building for the juice. There are two that sell fruit juice, but they were swarming over them all."

"Tylenol," Caroline said, head back, eyes closed.

"They'd like that."

Purely random poisonings, no specific targets, Peter and now Valerie accidental values for the variable: to whom it might concern. Could it be?

Chapter Eight

1

Lillie professed to be worried that Herb would be next.

"I don't drink fruit juice."

"It's good for you."

"Tell it to Peter and Valerie."

But he did not feel up to another eulogy. Imagine him saying the last words at Peter Kessel's memorial. It should have been the reverse. What would Peter have said of him? What would anyone have said of Herbert Laplace? He imagined himself in a box and Rogerson at the podium talking about his old friend Herb Laplace. Friend? He wouldn't put it past that bastard to dance on his grave.

He thought of it driving to his office through the gray November morning. *I have no friends*. Was that true? What is a friend? He decided that all his real friends had preceded him into death, and why should he care what any survivor said of him?

But he did care. Herb realized that he was really not that indifferent to the decent opinion of mankind. Or womankind. Crap. Mankind meant both. What if Lillie ended up with the last word? My God.

Rose was making the coffee when he got there and obviously wanted to talk about what had happened to Valerie. It would have to wait.

"I've got a nine o'clock meeting. Bellini, Mayhew, Huile and Harrigan, the comptroller. We'll need that coffee."

He went on into his office and shut the door. He stood with his back against it and looked around the room. How he loved it. It had been his, he had tossed it away on bad advice, but now it was his again, if only temporarily. He had to hang on to it. There had to be a way.

Yesterday he had gotten through to Bancroft Danto after more than a week of trying. Speaking assignments were drying up and Danto had delayed production of the album.

"The numbers don't look good, Herb. If it was up to me alone, I'd say go ahead. But I need a more promising prospect than seems to be developing."

"So there'll be no album?"

"I'm not saying that, Herb. What I'm saying is that at this point in time it does not look as strong as I had hoped. I don't recommend that you go out and roll another car or anything, but the truth is the public is fickle. A few months ago, you were hot. The alcoholic chancellor. The educator who snapped under pressure. It was a great gimmick."

Herb felt used. He had been sweet talked by too many people in the aftermath of his mistake. First to resign, then to go on the circuit like one of the Watergate crowd. He should be so lucky.

"How much have I earned?"

"I can have the figures drawn up, Herb."

"When do I get it?"

"If you will check your contract, Herb, you will see we use the same schedule as a publisher paying royalties. Your earnings are computed twice a year and paid within three months."

Danto had provided him with airline tickets, the hotels were covered by his hosts, he was reimbursed for other expenses by Danto's office. But apart from the money he had received on signing, he had yet to see the fabulous sums he supposed he had earned. Lillie didn't believe he wasn't rich. They quarreled about it. That was one of the reasons he called Danto yesterday.

Now, safe in his office again, Herb Laplace realized he had no alternative to this job. He *had* to fight for it. And the chances of his keeping it looked better than ever.

It was sad about Peter and Valerie and he had meant every word he said over Peter's ashes but it took an effort to imagine Peter taking over. Valerie? He shook his head. There was little danger that he would be asked to speak her eulogy, but he was more than willing to do it.

The clock read 8:45, time for a short session in the Barcalounger. He sat and got parallel with the floor and stared at the stippled ceiling above him. What a tale of woe the last months had been. Had it been months since he got the news of Norah Vlach? Events were a blur.

When things were going right, when people thought he could get them things they wanted, Herb was flattered and deferred to. He had told himself he had no illusions about the motives of those fawning over him, but in his heart he had thought they meant it. How could they not love him? Well, his run-in with the cops in Morton had revealed things as they really were. People hated his guts. Most people, anyway. Who didn't? Rogerson? He should have asked that Rogerson be invited to this meeting. Better him than that yo-yo Herman whose head looked like a kneecap.

Bellini came at five of nine, and then Mayhew and the others on the hour. Bellini took Herb's desk without apology. There was a single item on the agenda. How to stop the hemorrhaging.

"Restore me to office," Herb said.

Bellini looked around. Ollie Huile spoke.

"After what's been going on around here lately, a little turn at a massage parlor in Morton looks almost innocent."

"It was," Herb said.

"The drinking wasn't," Harrigan said. What a prick he was. His unit had been computerized to a fare-thee-well, but he still looked like someone out of Dickens, just slipped off his stool to come to this meeting.

"It doesn't matter," said Bellini. "I already talked to the governor. He thinks we made a fool of him on the Kessel matter."

"Does he think we killed Peter?" Mayhew asked.

"His point is we should have been more concerned about Peter's illness that morning. I told him you thought Peter was hung over. He didn't like that." He glanced at Herb. "He said don't give me another one of those."

"Tell it to the ethics committee," Herb snarled.

Twice, while he was a member of the state legislature, Watson, now the governor, had been investigated by that body's ethics committee, the second time for putting undue pressure on the ethics committee the first time.

"I agree with Herb," Mayhew said. "His resigning caused far more problems than it solved."

"Thank you, Gil."

"Speaking professionally," Huile said, "it's a piece of cake."

Bellini shook his head. "He won't go for it."

"What the hell does he want?"

"He wants a list of the names the search committee has come up with."

"Abe should be here," Harrigan said.

"Abe's name is on the list."

"The way things are going, his will be the only one left."

"Those pieces in the local paper were picked up in Columbus."

Caroline Swift had been lyrical about the democratic device of a search committee appointed by the Faculty Senate. Of course, she had gone on to make Valerie Kraft the obvious ultimate choice.

"Watson likes the idea of that committee more and more. It takes him off the hook."

"Herman should be here," Harrigan repeated.

"Does he want a vote taken?"

"It looks like the best way, Herb."

Laplace's heart sank. Where would he be now if his career had depended on the votes of his colleagues? He had become assistant dean by flattering his predecessor and then dean by exposing the man's incompetence to Wooley the president. He had reached the top after wheeling and dealing in Columbus. It was dizzying to think that now his future depended on the whims and resentments of the faculty he had ruled for nearly a decade.

2

Rogerson went to the daily mass at St. Casimer's. The seven-thirty was said by old Lezcenski, a cadaverous Pole who said mass swiftly but with complete absorption and devotion. No eye contact, no personal variations in the canon, no kiss of peace, as the Rotary Club handshaking and general milling around before the Agnus Dei were still called. That is why he didn't notice Carlotta until he was leaving the church.

"You're right," she said. "This isn't the Newman chapel."

"The polar opposite."

"Is there a Latin mass?"

"Once a month. The six A.M. on Sunday is in Polish for the old folks."

And not only for the old folks. Last Sunday, arriving early for the seven, Rogerson had been surprised at the range of ages emerging from the church. What a shot in the arm John Paul II had been.

Today at the commemoration for the dead, Rogerson added the names of Peter and Valerie to the lengthening list of those he had survived. Would either have wanted prayers? There were others on his list who would have said, alive, no thanks. Presumably they were all of a different mind now.

How odd his own faith was came home to him when he saw it mirrored in those around him. Cast a cold anthropologist's eye, or psychologist's eye, or just about any eye but the eye of faith on what they were doing, and it would seem a strange remnant from a surpassed stage of the race. But looked at from the believer's point of view, it was unbelievable that others did not see the ultimate point of life.

Rogerson stopped by police headquarters later. Ennis was not happy to see him. Both Peter and Valerie had been killed by arsenic poisoning, Ennis reported, one dose, in both cases very likely administered with fruit juice.

"They found a plastic carton in his trash. There were traces of arsenic."

"Fingerprints?"

"Just his."

That both should have been killed in the same way certainly suggested the same killer, but what beside the method linked the two?

"The search for a new chancellor," Rogerson said, completing the detective's thought.

"That, yes. And also they were both administrators who had left teaching."

"Who were in the running for chancellor."

"But so are others. *You* are."

"I have an alibi." It seemed important to confirm Ennis's apparent view of professors.

"Are there any other candidates who have abandoned the classroom?"

"Herb Laplace," Rogerson said.

"He should be warned," Ennis said.

What the police were doing was systematically going through the effects of the two victims. Enid, Peter's secretary, was making a list of those who might have had a particular grievance against the assistant to the chancellor.

What an infinity of possibly relevant facts there was, Rogerson reflected. No wonder justice was such a chancy thing. It seemed a matter of eliminating possibilities, but that still left an infinity of others.

"None of the other cartons in the vending machines contained arsenic," Ennis said.

"So it isn't random."

Ennis concluded that the juice was brought to them. Presumably by the same person. Find that person and that's the end of it.

Rogerson had a class at 2:15.

"Why is there anything rather than nothing?" he asked, and the question carried him effortlessly through fifty minutes. Not why do oaks come from acorns and tan flesh from lying in the sun nor why do fish gotta swim and birds gotta fly, but why does this whole set of things exist at all?

Most of the class gaped at him, some napped, others stared without wonder out the window at lowering skies and an imagined freedom, a young man named Guggenheim was poised on the edge of his chair determined to ask a question if Rogerson relented and looked at him, Amanda Davis sat bolt upright in the back row following every word with riveted eyes. She stayed right there until everyone but Guggenheim had left and then came with Rogerson as he left the room.

"How do you spell Leibniz?"

"The same way he did."

The memorable smile did not appear. She waited. He spelled it for her. He could not remember Leibniz's first name. "Let's go look it up."

What he wanted to do was go to his office and have a cup of coffee and a cigarette. They could look up Leibniz's first name there.

"What do you mean by nothing?" she asked, puffing at her bangs.

"What's left when you take everything away."

Her nose wrinkled. "That's nuts."

"You may be right."

"You'd have to take away yourself."

"Right."

"So who's the nothing nothing for?"

"God."

"Then there's still something."

"God isn't just another thing. He's everything."

Before going to his office he stopped for his mail. He introduced Amanda to Julie the departmental secretary who had a thick Sidney Sheldon paperback closed on her finger.

"Professor Rogerson is the candidate of the Independent Students Association," Amanda said.

"A philosopher king!" Wiley the chairman cried from his office. He had pushed his chair away from his desk, tilting it back, and looked out at them as if ready for the dentist.

"If I survive. Candidates are currently an endangered species."

There were racks of the student newspaper along the campus walks and he took a copy. So did Amanda. She opened it and handed it to Rogerson. It was her story on Valerie Kraft's press conference.

3

She had not had to look on Peter dead but when Sylvia called her from Valerie's office and half-hysterically begged her to come at once, Carlotta went at once and there was the lifeless Valerie slumped over her desk. It was the first time Carlotta had seen unadorned death, death before it is softened by the undertaker's art. When her parents died she had not been at their side and saw them only later at the wake. She surprised herself by putting her hand gently on Valerie's forehead. It was a cold unlike any she had felt before.

"She's dead," Sylvia said, her thin voice employing a single vocal string.

"Have you called anyone?"

Sylvia nodded. She could not tear her eyes from the slack dead face of Valerie.

"The campus police."

"After you called me?"

"Just before you came. I've been in the hallway. I didn't want to be alone with her."

But Sylvia was alone when the police did come, the real police, summoned by the campus Keystone Cops because Sylvia had mentioned a body. Carlotta was in the Ladies and when she emerged to find Sylvia babbling to half a dozen uniformed and ununiformed cops at once she did a cowardly thing. She slipped away.

Sylvia did not know what had happened to Valerie and Carlotta knew even less, but it might take hours to convince the police of that. Walking the campus in a kind of daze, oblivious to the unlighted areas she normally would have avoided at this hour of night, she repeated over and over to herself, Valerie is dead, Peter is dead, Valerie is dead, Peter is dead. If she had meant this mental chanting to emphasize the utter uniqueness of these truths, she would have been disappointed. *Repetitio est mater studiorum*. A phrase of Peter's. But repetition deadens awareness, domesticates what is repeated, robs signs of their significance. She might have been praying, her mind was so little engaged.

From the open windows of the student dorms rock music blasted, dozens of warring chaoses, driving thought away. Carlotta felt suspended between the students and the faculty, in her mind belonging to neither. At twenty-nine she was older than the students and younger than her colleagues. When she talked of Tolstoy to her class she had the sense of letting the young in on the folly of adults.

In a life of Dostoyevsky she had recently taken from the library there was a photograph of the writer just after he died. He looked like a drawing about to be erased. Peter had been reduced to ashes and it took an act of faith to think of him contained in the urn displayed during the ceremony. If she rubbed it, would he reappear? Valerie looked like the dead Dostoyevsky.

The face of death repelled her, frightened her, filled her with awe. The one thing she did not feel was grief. Shock, no doubt, but when she went back to her car and hesitated, thinking she should go inside again and give Sylvia moral support, she rejected the idea. Here was one effect of the presence of death. She felt isolated, alone, deadened.

The reason she could not feel grief, could not cry, was that this was more than death. Peter and Valerie had been killed. By any natural estimate, both of them had had years of life ahead. To think of them as dead was to ask who had killed them.

And why.

It had truly come as a surprise to Carlotta that people of the intelligence of Peter and Valerie wanted to be chancellor of this place. Wanted! They had lusted for it. Not even Peter had been able to joke about it, although he did a wonderful imitation of Laplace whom he clearly regarded as a fool. And Valerie had held Handel in contempt. Of course, Valerie despised all men, at least she claimed to.

Who poisoned them? How natural it was to assume they had been killed because they wanted to be chancellor. When Peter was found dead, it had occurred to Carlotta that Valerie would have wanted her rival out of the way. The thought had not risen to the level of suspicion, but now Valerie was exonerated by becoming a victim herself.

The four rooms of Carlotta's apartment still struck her as almost obscenely too many. The cramp and austerity of the room she'd had in Moscow when she studied there had provided a scale. Standing in the bedroom, she remembered the morning Valerie had called and Peter answered the phone.

And now both were dead. Briefly, so briefly, there was the promise of tears. The telephone rang.

Carlotta stared at it. It was absurd to think it was Valerie calling, but she hesitated to answer. Finally, she did, briskly, sweeping up the instrument and saying a crisp hello.

"Carlotta?"

It was Sylvia, her voice even more strained than before.

"Sylvia, I'm sorry . . ."

"Thank God you're all right. I thought . . . I don't know what I thought. I'll be right there. Carlotta, the police are on their way."

"The police?"

"I'll explain."

Only minutes after she hung up, the doorbell rang. They were a team, a male and a female half a head taller than the male, she bulging with leather and metal and herself, the badge brazen on her breast. Valerie would never have forgiven her for thinking the woman cop looked make-believe.

"Everything okay here?"

"Of course."

The male said, "Mind if we come inside?"

"There's no reason for that. I'm perfectly fine. Nothing is wrong."

The two cops looked at each other. The woman produced a pad from her hip.

"We have to ask you a few questions."

They were still there when Sylvia arrived, bursting in like Brünhilde and taking Carlotta in her arms, sobbing aloud. The cops shuffled in embarrassment.

After the police left, Caroline Swift came. She had been at the provost's office when Sylvia had suddenly realized Carlotta was missing. In the circumstances the fact seemed ominous.

"I went for a walk on campus."

"At night!" Night or day, Sylvia could not escape notice, blond, blessed in body and mind, her pale, blue-eyed stare that of a lioness out of Blake.

"Who poisoned Valerie?" Caroline demanded.

"I am going to have a glass of wine."

They drank a bottle and a half among them, Sylvia taking more than her share. After the third glass she announced that she did not intend to swim in the morning. Caroline put a piece of paper on the coffee table and made a list of suspects and victims.

"They are not exclusive lists, of course."

Victims, actual and possible, were candidates for the chancellorship. It seemed absurd when she wrote down Rogerson.

"And Laplace, I suppose," Carlotta said.

"He's first of the suspects."

Herb Laplace as assassin? But when assassination meant putting arsenic in fruit juice, it was something even a coward could do.

"Abe Herman," Carlotta suddenly remembered. "Abe should be on the list too."

"Which list?"

"Both."

4

There was only one name on Abe Herman's list of candidates for the chancellorship, and that name was his own.

Other candidates dropping like flies should have made a mockery of his ambition, but what else was there? Besides, someone had to run this place, and Abe felt the burden settling on his own shoulders.

To whom did others turn in the confusion of these days? Abe Herman. Last night, going on one A.M., he had received a somewhat drunken call from Carlotta. Of course he had heard about Valerie. The police had been with him for an hour. And he had been in conference with Mayhew. As soon as it was decent, after they got Valerie into the ground, he would call a meeting of the search committee, suggest the convening of the full senate, and force a vote on the remaining candidates. He had little doubt about what the outcome would be.

He thought this dispassionately. The future would simply be this, being in charge, directing the flow, leading. Even Laplace had called him.

"They got Valerie, huh?"

"They?"

"The forces of evil," Herb said, almost angrily. Abe's retort had deflected the chumminess. He regretted that.

"They'll get us all in the end, Herb."

"Not me they won't. I'm a survivor."

God knew there was truth to that. Only a few months ago, Laplace was on the ropes, publicly nailed as a drunk and frequenter of massage parlors. Of course this endeared him to the students for whom previously he had been a distant ogre, but the sonofabitch had then snatched complete victory from the jaws of defeat, and cleaned up on the road telling avid audiences what a sonofabitch he was—and so would they be if they didn't watch out. Amazing. More amazing still, Herb was still ensconced in the chancellor's office.

That had seemed a solution once, Herb keeping the place open because no one would think of him as permanently there. No one? The uneasy thought came that Herb's staying right where he was for good might also seem a solution. Abe would have to bring himself to the forefront now.

Which is why, when his phone rang at seven-thirty in the morning, a disheveled Abe Herman stifled his anger and told Amanda Davis he would be happy to give her an interview for the campus paper.

"I'll be in my office in forty-five minutes."

"I'm calling from the Marquette Mall." In the neighborhood. "I'd like to get the story in today."

"Be here in fifteen minutes."

She was there in ten and he was still running the electric razor over his face when he opened the door and looked out over the chain at the woebegone student. Too late it occurred to him that this was a bad time to have a girl in his apartment. But he let her in.

There was momentary reassurance when she stood inside the door, hitching her bag up on her shoulder, ducking her head, pigeon-toed. Another sort of alarm went off in his head. Beware the wounded bird.

"I'm still having breakfast. Want coffee?"

"Thanks."

She followed him into the kitchen where she lowered her bag to the floor with one hand and took a notebook from the pocket of her topcoat with the other.

"Want to take off your coat?"

"It's okay." She unbuttoned it, however, and Abe turned away. It seemed a provocative act. Again he felt a special danger in this girl. Amanda. The kind that clings, that whines, that wants her daddy back again.

"How long have you written for the paper?"

"Just this semester."

He put a cup of coffee across the table from his own and they sat.

With one foot, she moved her bag closer. She laid the notebook flat on the table.

"Why isn't Professor Rogerson taken seriously as candidate for chancellor?"

"I thought you wanted to talk about Dr. Kraft's death."

"The Independent Students are quite serious about Professor Rogerson."

"Do you know him?"

"Yes."

"How well?"

"I am taking a course from him."

"Can you imagine him running this place?"

"Oh, yes."

"I don't think he would want to, Amanda."

"I don't blame him. But he could change it."

"That's true."

"You don't think so."

He wished she did not lean toward him when she spoke. He felt intimidated by her fervor.

"If people keep getting poisoned, Rogerson will be the only one left."

5

Still abed at seven-thirty, Rogerson knew he'd have to forego St. Casimir's this morning. He had been up late the night before, reading, and he rolled over now in the hope of recapturing sleep. But it eluded, as objects of desire often did. After twenty minutes he gave up. He sat on the edge of the bed and combed his beard with the fingers of his left hand. With his right he brushed the hair from his eyes and thought of Amanda Davis.

Strange girl. Her campaign promoting him for chancellor had been more amusing when he thought she realized how futile it was.

"It's the highest position, isn't it?" she asked.

"And the lowest form of life."

"You'll be a good chancellor."

Perhaps if his morning mind were clearer there would not have been the random conjunction of events and statements that filled him with unease.

Ennis apparently assumed that a candidate for chancellor was getting rid of the opposition, but he seemed to have no genuine theory. The police collected information, wrote reports, interviewed the same people again and again, came to no conclusions. Fort Elbow seemed to be a fairly safe city for a murderer. Maybe most cities were.

"It sounds logical," Rogerson admitted.

"I haven't let you out of my sight," Ennis said with a slight smile.

"It could be someone with a passionate interest in one of the candidates."

"Passionate."

"Not all passion is sexual."

Now, sitting on the edge of his bed, thinking of Amanda and her odd determination, he wished he had mentioned her to Ennis.

Rogerson got to his feet and shuffled to the study where he looked up Abe Herman's phone number and dialed it. The ringing began and continued. No answer. He put down the phone.

He wanted to call Ennis, but first he tried Herman's office number. He got no answer there either.

Ennis answered on the first ring. "I think you should check immediately on Abe Herman."

"Why?"

"He doesn't answer his phone."

"Where does he live?"

Rogerson gave Ennis the address.

"Where is Mansfield Court?"

Some cop. Rogerson told him.

"What are we looking for?"

"A live candidate."

"Where you calling from?"

Rogerson hung up and called 911 and said that paramedics were needed in Mansfield Court. He had half a mind to drive to Abe's apartment himself.

Rogerson's car was a rusted-out Omega, ten years old, beautiful lines, what was left of them. Maybe if he had been dressed he would have gone. In any case, Amanda Davis was coming up his walk.

Before he let her in he answered the phone.

6

The arsenic was in the bag she wore slung over her shoulder, but it would be well over half an hour before he asked her if it was. She squinted at him, lifting a hand to clear a line of sight through her bangs, but did not immediately answer. She worked her lips as if she had just applied lipstick, but he doubted she ever used it.

"How did you know?"

"The police just called from Professor Herman's apartment."

"What are they doing there?"

"They got there in time."

This had the effect of relaxing her. She opened her bag and put a jar on the table and they both looked at it.

"You're a chemistry major," he said.

"Death isn't a big deal."

"I've never died."

One corner of her mouth dimpled slightly. "I mean it. It's just a change. People go on somewhere else."

"I believe that, too."

"So what I did wasn't so terrible."

"There I disagree with you."

"So will the police. I know that. But what can they do to me, put me to death? Death isn't a big deal."

"I don't think you can count on death in Ohio."

"Maybe they won't catch me."

"They will be talking with Professor Herman."

"He didn't see me do it."

She took the jar and put it back into her purse. Rogerson didn't try to stop her. There was no way she could escape from what she had done.

"There's coffee on."

"Herman offered me coffee, too."

"I'll keep an eye on you."

"Last week in one of my classes we talked about *Crime and Punishment*. Did you ever read it?"

"What did you make of it?"

"We talked of Raskolnikov's theory of murder. The gratuitous act."

"He ended up in Siberia."

"Did he?"

"He experienced a religious conversion. Dostoyevsky was a very religious man."

"I believe in another world."

"It's not the same thing."

She took the coffee he poured for her and watched him lower himself onto the couch.

"How long have you lived here?"

"I hate to think."

"We never lived in the same place two years in a row."

They talked on, aimlessly, and Rogerson was impressed by her illiteracy. Whatever native talent she had, her education had not engaged it. She seemed to think Dostoyevsky and Tolstoy were still alive in Russia. Of Christianity she had less knowledge than the Huns before Boniface came. Yet she had been raised a Christian.

"We were Methodists."

"Were?"

"My father used to say that long after Christianity had disappeared from the face of the earth the Methodist church would go on."

Rogerson laughed.

"We quit when he found out his contributions were arming Marxist revolutionaries."

"Is that true?"

"He thought it was."

"So he left."

She held her coffee in both hands. She had murdered two people and tried to murder a third, but it had left no mark on her because death was no big deal.

"I prefer mysticism. Do you know Zen?"

"Do you know Teresa of Avila?"

She had never heard of Saint Teresa but her mind was filled with oddments of Eastern mysticism. She doubted the body was real and that people are meant to be individuals.

"In the end we'll all end up as one."

She surprised him when she suddenly began to gag. Good Lord! What an idiot he was. How had she managed to get the arsenic into her coffee without his seeing her? Her cunning almost got her into the next life she said she believed in. His call to 911 brought the paramedics and a screaming patrol car. Ennis arrived just as they were taking her away. She was still alive, but Rogerson doubted she would continue to think death was no big deal.

Chapter Nine

1

Rain fell and turned to snow and the campus buildings stood like whited sepulchers among the leafless trees. Students jackknifed into the wind or sailed before it with their coats pasted to their backs. There was the whine of tires on ice, the roar of snow blowers, the sky was shades of gray. There are many smaller worlds within the world, and here was one of them—but even on this diminished stage the question of the new chancellor had lost what zest it had.

Amanda Davis recovered from the arsenic she had taken and was in custody for a couple of weeks until she was judged incompetent to stand trial. Off she then went to the hospital for the criminally insane, from which at least once a day she wrote a long, eerily coherent letter to Professor Rogerson assuring him that he alone could save the university.

Rogerson, slipping and sliding to class, his wool cap pulled low on his forehead, mucus freezing in his mustache, squinted at the passing students. In the lounge he attended to what his colleagues had to say. More than ever before in his long career he felt he had been deposited in a parody of higher education.

The student newspaper was aflame with articles about the

promised football team. Debates raged on the name to be given the squad, the site of the stadium, possible opponents. The Akron University Zips offered to put the new team on their schedule. All this was premature but the issue was the only one that interested Bellini. Herb had announced he wanted his old job back.

"Fielding a football team is a dream I have had for years," he said solemnly. "I want to be chancellor when that great day arrives."

"What's taken so long?" the student reporter asked.

"Politics. Fortunately, Senator Bellini is leading the battle now and victory is assured."

"Didn't he play football?"

"You may be right."

"The name sounds familiar."

"He is our state senator."

"I think he played for the Rams."

The reporter had hollow cheeks, a large nose and a dimpled if receding chin. He was assistant sports editor. He wrote in a ringed notebook with the number two Ticonderoga pencil Laplace had given him when his ballpoint wouldn't work.

"Maybe it's invisible ink," Herb suggested.

"If I press down hard enough I can read it later, but it's not easy."

Herb gave him the pencil. "Did you know Amanda Davis?"

"Amanda Davis."

"The girl who poisoned the professors."

"She was a special reporter."

"She sure was."

Herb's stand on the football team made him a popular man with the paper. Once there was a letter signed "Curious" asking what the status of Chancellor Laplace's trial for drunken driving was, but the editor lamented in an appended note the pusillanimity of the letter writer.

Pusillanimity? Herb looked it up, it sounded like a word he could use, but the definition amounted to synonyms—abjectness, cowardliness, contemptibility—and seemed to rob the word of its hissing significance. He tried it out on Rogerson to his sorrow.

"It's a long *u*, Herb."

"Say it."

"*U*."

"I meant the word."

"Someone showed me that letter."

"You sure you didn't write it?"

"It sounds like Amanda."

"What a yo-yo. You were the only one safe from her. I'm surprised they didn't lock you up as an accomplice."

"Is that coffee you're drinking?"

"Would you like some?"

"I don't dare."

"Ho ho." But Herb pushed his cooling cup away. Some days he thought of how easy it would be for a student to get him. Amanda Davis was not an isolated case. Every semester Psychological Services got a predictable quota of deranged scholars. Resentment modulated with the seasons but early winter was a bad time. They were inching toward the Thanksgiving break and none too soon. Last week there had been a suicide in one of the women's residences. Pregnant. In the paper a counselor lamented this senseless waste of life. The girl could have had an abortion easily.

It was the kind of publicity they did not need. Bellini's opponents in Columbus could do a lot with a knocked-up co-ed. During this chancy time Rogerson withdrew his own name and endorsed Herb for chancellor, saying that he couldn't think of a better man for the job.

Herb was moved and called Matt to tell him so.

"Did you take that as flattery, Herb?"

Good old Rogerson. "I appreciate your saying it, Matt. You're a pal."

Lillie thought so too. "Remember who your real friends are, Herbert."

Her words would have sounded wiser if she hadn't been long gone in the sauce when she said them. Lillie was still devastated by the collapse of the dreams he had encouraged in her with Bancroft Danto's lies. Of course, Lillie assumed he had already stashed away great sums. She lived in the dread—or hope, he couldn't decide which—that he would one day abandon her. But the half he had planned to squirrel away proved as phantom as the rest.

"Our books are open to client inspection at any time, Herb," Danto said blandly when he phoned about the statement showing that everything Danto owed him was canceled by what he allegedly owed the agent.

"Do you mean I broke my butt all those weeks in order to break even?"

"If your engagements had continued on the line shown by the first three weeks, you would have been in clover."

"You told me I already was."

"On the basis of those projections."

"You were going to put half in a Cleveland account."

"Half of what was owed you, yes."

"Half of zilch?"

"After the first of the year, we can try putting you on the road again, Herb. It would help if you could get into the news."

"How about getting reappointed chancellor?"

"That might help." But Danto sounded dubious.

But the attraction of getting the job back was to free himself from leeches like Danto.

"Let's move," Herb urged Bellini.

"What do you mean?"

"Under the circumstances, a quiet, dignified press release would do it. Herbert Laplace has been named to resume his post as chancellor of the Fort Elbow campus, et cetera, et cetera. People want the thing settled. Let me read you a statement by Rogerson."

"Rogerson!"

"It makes sense."

What a memory the guy had. In meetings, Rogerson constantly referred to the senator as Ballerina. Thank God, he hadn't mentioned him in speaking to the student reporter. Didn't he play football? Sure, without a helmet. Bellini began to grumble about the spot Peter Kessel's death had put him in. The governor had a long memory, too. He felt he had been led down the garden path once on the chancellorship and he didn't intend to have it happen again.

"Stage an election," Bellini suggested.

"An election?"

"Fort Elbow faculty selects So-and-so. That takes everybody off the hook."

"A referendum?"

"You want the students in on it, go ahead."

My God. What he wanted was what he had asked for, the appointment.

"You win that vote and you'll be appointed, Herb. That's the best I can do."

"I thought you wanted football on this campus."

There was a pause. "You want to bargain?"

"Why not?"

"You got nothing to bargain with."

"Maybe, maybe not. You think anyone else is going to help you get that team?"

"Professor Herman says he thinks football would be great for student morale."

"He told you that?"

"He told the press that, or so I hear."

Bellini was right. Abe Herman of all people, the great foe of student athletics, allowed that the American university was unimaginable without both intramural and varsity sports and preeminent among the latter was football. In these days of the NCAA it was difficult to remember that it was in the Ivy League that college football first flourished and rose to national attention. Among Aristotle's lesser-known achievements was a list of winners of the Olympic Games. What was good enough for the Ivy League and Aristotle was certainly good enough for Abe Herman.

"Words," Laplace said disdainfully to Bellini.

"Recorded words. He might try to welsh on me, but not on the students."

The implication was clear. Bellini had himself covered with either Laplace or Herman. Moreover, the governor had expressed willingness to appoint the faculty's choice. There was no escaping it. An election was the only way Herb Laplace could regain his old job.

2

Abe Herman's victim status made him the darling of campus pressure groups. A stern and stocky student, apparently female, assured Abe that he was the candidate of the Gay/Lesbian Coalition.

"We've got Women's Studies, right?"

"Ours was one of the first programs in the state," he assured his visitor.

"We've got Black Studies."

"We do, indeed."

"Why not Gay/Lesbian Studies?"

"Interesting."

She leaned forward and sailed some papers onto his desk. "That's all I've been able to collect on programs in other schools."

"There would have to be faculty approval."

"Sure."

The spokesman for the Edmund Burke Society was equally blunt.

"We want our office back in Ambrose Bierce Hall."

"I don't understand." All approved student groups were eligible for office space in Bierce.

"Secure offices. The reason we moved out was that we were always being broken into." He was over six feet tall, wore a three-piece suit and tasteful tie, and his hair was slicked back. The black onyx ring he kept twisting was impressive. One day this boy would be an honor to the school.

"What is your major, Williams?"

"Political Science."

"Ah. What are your career plans?"

"Professor Herman, at the moment my interests are centered on this campus. We want a chancellor who is genuinely interested in pluralism."

They all came to his door eventually and he promised them the moon. Why not? Unless he became chancellor he could do nothing for the campus. Talking with representatives of the pressure groups, he dreamed of a campus where students were more interested in panning nuggets of knowledge from the stream of curricular offerings—he jotted that down, he would use it in his inaugural address—than anticipating the pleasures of later life. What this place needed was more cold showers and an honor code.

It hurt that Rogerson, his rescuer, was backing Laplace and he told Matt so.

"You have many years before you, Abe. May your declension be gradual and slow. You aren't corrupt enough yet for academic administration. There are still vestiges of decency in your soul, you still *have* some soul. Herb, on the other hand, well, I think of him as an old and practiced streetwalker. You can't seduce a prostitute, right?"

"I can do things for this school, Matt."

"Please. No threats."

Carlotta and Sylvia had visited him in the hospital, had stood on either side of his bed and looked down sadly at him. He felt he was anticipating his own wake. He closed his eyes. He could be dead. If that crazy girl had succeeded, he would now be a fading memory.

That Rogerson had called the police and paramedics had been summoned, that they were told immediately to treat him for arsenic poisoning—on such improbable threads as these his life had hung. His heart was swollen with gratitude, but Rogerson deflected any expression of it.

"It was just a matter of making a few illogical leaps."

"You saved my life."

"I apologize."

Abe leaned toward him and touched his arm.

"Do you know the passage in Plato, Abe?"

Socrates suggested that those saved from shipwreck might live to curse their rescuer. How could they know what future trials he had preserved them for?

In Sylvia's sympathetic eyes, Abe thought he saw thoughts of Peter Kessel, just as Carlotta seemed to be thinking of Valerie. The significance of their gaze was clear. He too might have gone to that bourne from which no traveler returns. Abe himself had lost whatever belief in immortality he once had. Any future he expected was terrestrial and, God help him, on this campus. He meant to make the most of it.

Once out of the hospital, he had learned either to curry sympathy with the ravaged look of a nearly poisoned man or to exude the efficient optimism of one eager to lead this campus into the next century, depending on the circumstances. When he spoke with Bellini he used both.

"How'd it feel to almost die?" the senator asked.

"I don't recommend it."

"I've read about it. People who died and came back. What did you see?"

What would Bellini like to hear? "What did the others say?"

Bellini sat back and looked at the ceiling. He was thinking. He dropped his chin. He had it.

"Light. They said it was like coming out of a dark room into a brightly lighted room."

Abe nodded with pursed lips as the senator spoke. This was a new side of Bellini. Thoughts of mortality were heavy in his eyes.

"That's about right. Did they mention the music?"

It was shameless but Abe fed Bellini's desire to know what lay beyond the grim boundary separating the quick from the dead.

Willie Wainwright, a local preacher whose sermons had just been taken up by a cable network, looked into Abe's hospital room, a limp Bible clutched to his bosom, and smiled.

"Everything all right, Brother?"

Everything got better all the time. He was on his feet and back to work and Bellini accepted the suggestion of an election.

"I don't have to explain the importance of elections to you, Senator."

"Good God, no." Bellini shut his eyes at the reminder of all those unknown jackasses sealing his fate on election day.

"There'd be an uproar if a new chancellor is just dumped on us from on high. It's gruesome to say, Senator Bellini, but Peter Kessel's death spared you a lot of flak."

"There won't be an appointment from on high."

"The election can't be just an exercise."

The governor, he was told, was willing to appoint the person democratically chosen by the faculty.

"Does Laplace know that?"

Bellini looked at his watch, a massive thing with multiple dials strapped and buckled to his wrist like a championship belt.

"I'm going to see him in ten minutes."

3

"Why?" Carlotta asked.

"Because he's cynical. And old. Matt Rogerson won't have to live with the result, at least not very long."

"Laplace is as old as Matt."

"Really?"

"Sixty-two."

Sylvia was a little older than Carlotta and sixty-two didn't completely slip off the scale for her. Matt was nearly thirty years older than she was. Ten years ago that had mattered less. Having a wife had kept him young.

Was that true? Or would he have aged so much even if his wife had lived? He talked of retiring, but that's all it was, talk. "Lord, to whom would we go?" So he had mused aloud once, talking about it. A quote. Shakespeare, he said. She knew that wasn't right. So Carlotta's explanation didn't fit. Except the cynical part.

"He's the best man for the job," he told Sylvia when she asked him.

"Laplace? You despise Laplace."

"He is best fitted for the job."

"Oh, don't be cute, Matt. He was bad enough before. Imagine what he would be like if he was reinstated."

"He's been doing the job all along."

"When he's been in town."

Sylvia would vote for Abe Herman on December sixth, but not with a great deal of enthusiasm. She wanted promotion to full professor and it wouldn't hurt to be owed a favor by the new chancellor.

Carlotta said, "I'd like to vote for Rogerson."

"You'd have to write in his name."

The woman's fascination with Rogerson reminded Sylvia of her own when she was new on the faculty. She could remember ten years ago on this campus. Did she want to be here ten years from now? Compared with what, as the man said when asked how his wife was. A faint smile. Rogerson. Sometimes she would imagine his asking to marry her and her moving in with him. It would be about as romantic as moving in with Carlotta. Sylvia was happy enough, she liked the life she led, one week much like the last, teaching nine months a year, traveling and lazing around the rest. On

Christmas break she was going to San Miguel Allende, to relax and read, maybe a little adventure, though she would never have formulated that as part of the reason. Was it? Well, what the hell, she wasn't a nun. She wasn't cheating on anyone.

Sometimes the line of her life seemed to stretch ahead of her, going nowhere, just one damned thing after another. She blamed such dismal thoughts on Rogerson. He was contagious. Philosophers were all crazy, everybody knew that. And Rogerson was crazier than any other she had known.

"I have a nightmare that this campus is typical, no worse than most."

Matt seemed to expect her to contest this. She tended to think he was right. There were a few good universities, a dozen or so, and then there were the rest. Fort Elbow was no worse than the average add-on campus in a state system.

Maybe with Abe Herman as chancellor it would improve. Carlotta thought so. She looked forward to the faculty having a say in the direction the university took. Sylvia had been to enough departmental meetings to be skeptical about that. If she was for Abe, it was because she didn't want Herb Laplace back as chancellor. Eventually, Abe would become a pain in the neck too, but Laplace already was.

"Always go with the known evil," Rogerson advised.

"I'd love to. Pick me up at nine."

"I'll knock you down at eight."

"I like your proposition."

"McDonald's or Wendy's?"

4

Listening to Herman obliquely state his proposition, Handel felt the peculiar pleasure of one whose worst estimates of the times are proving true. *Delectatio morosa,* as one might say, but of course would not, not in these dark days when knowledge of Latin was a fading memory. Handel felt that way lately, Augustinian, call it a Gibbon mood. Laplace might call it Spenglerish. Handel thought of World War II songs his mother had sung when his father was fighting in the Pacific. *When the lights go on again* . . . An indirect way of saying they had all gone out.

"I know you'll agree that this university could be a lot better than it is," Herman said earnestly. How magnificently bald he was, the crown of his head like the Dome of the Rock.

"I can certainly agree with that." Who could not, for heaven's sake?

"There seems little logic in entrusting the direction of the school again to the man responsible for its present condition."

"Herb isn't all bad."

"No one is."

"He could be better than he is."

Herman smiled, an engaging smile. Handel liked him, despite his absurd ambition to be chancellor. Had he any idea how dreadful it was to be a bureaucrat?

"Once you offered me your support."

"So much has happened since then."

"I want your vote, Professor Handel."

"So, alas, does Laplace."

"Have you made up your mind?"

Handel thought wistfully that it would have been fun to vote for Matt Rogerson. Why, only weeks ago they'd had a lovely discussion of the *Glossa Ordinaria*. Did anyone else in the institution even know what it was? It wasn't a matter of snobbery, only of what one truly enjoyed.

The spirit of the conversation with Abe Herman prompted Handel to speak quite out of character as he recalled the pleasures of conversation with Rogerson.

"I will vote for you on one condition."

Herman moved forward on the cushion of his chair.

"Promise me that Matthew Rogerson will not be forced into early retirement."

"Done!"

Herman jumped to his feet and extended his hand. It might have been a holdup, but Handel felt that he had gotten the better of the situation. He shook Abe Herman's hand vigorously.

5

Normal perversity would have sufficed, but the skepticism of Sylvia Woods helped. Rogerson called Laplace and offered to meet the acting chancellor at a neutral site.

"What the hell does that mean?"

"Do you know the White Castle on Tamarack Trail?"

"Are they still in business?"

"Haven't you heard of the Albino Arches?"

Rogerson got there first and took two of the heel-shaped hamburgers and a cup of coffee to a corner booth. This place was a throwback to the thirties. Hamburgers five cents, take home a sackful. He remembered an identical structure on Wisconsin Avenue, himself nine years old, Depression boy, barefoot in bib overalls, selling the *Journal* for three cents at the corner and splurging later at the White Castle. He had reached the age when almost anything was a target of nostalgia.

"You a regular here?" Laplace said, sitting down across from him.

"Eat here and you will be regular."

"What's this about?"

"The election."

Laplace sat back. "You're selling out."

"I already have. I'm supporting you."

"I appreciate that."

"You're going to lose."

"Bullshit."

"Abe Herman is doing very well with the junior faculty. He even got Handel."

"Handel!" Laplace looked as Napoleon would look if he had learned of the treachery of Ney.

"I think I can get him back."

"How?"

"Let him remain active until he is seventy."

"He isn't active now."

"Yes or no?"

"Yes. I'll tell him myself."

"No. He'd have a nervous breakdown. Let me handle it."

"So with his vote you think I'll win?"

"No. Here's a statement for you to issue to the press."

Herb exploded when he read the first sentences. He tossed the sheet across the table. "Not on your life. Students voting? Matt, this is bad enough as is. Whose idea was this?"

"You announce you want students voting as well as faculty and what does Abe Herman do?"

"Agree?"

"Never. He's ambitious but he isn't an idiot. His reason will be—I will suggest this to him—that the student body turns over too rapidly and it would be wrong to give such power to youngsters who happen to be on the campus now. All too soon, they will be gone."

Laplace nodded. "Exactly."

"And that is your opening."

"Opening? I agree."

"Then you demand that only tenured faculty be allowed to vote. We propose this to the senate, where it must be acted on, and the senate is made up prepronderantly of tenured faculty."

"But how can you cut out faculty members?"

"On the same principle by which the students are excluded. There is no certainty that they will have to live with the result of their choice. The tenured faculty is the principle of stability in the university. The senate will like that. They will vote it through."

"And I get elected?"

"No. Then you have a chance. The junior faculty hates your guts."

"So does the tenured faculty."

"True. But you, in the phrase, are *our* sonofabitch. Who knows what power will do to Abe?"

Herb's announcement, written by his ad hoc campaign manager, appeared, Abe reacted almost exactly as predicted, adding that the students would still be settling in after Thanksgiving, and Rogerson introduced the motion in the senate. Abe took it like a man.

"You snookered me, Matt."

"Abe, if you are elected, I will be the first to congratulate you. But Herb needs the work."

"Ha. The bastard's rich."

Rogerson wondered. Herb was no longer off on lecture junkets and mumbled incoherently when asked about Bancroft Danto. Along with Matt, he spent his days lobbying the tenured faculty. Not all tenured professors were eligible for the Old Bastards, but anyone who had willingly accepted a permanent position on this campus was in no position to be picky about Herb Laplace. A proposal to have emeriti eligible to vote was defeated narrowly in the senate. Felix Freeman's first telegram from Phoenix was refused, but he translated it into a species of French and it got through. *"Quelle merde. Vive le vieux bâtard Laplace, c'est-à-dire, le lieu, ou comme disent nos frères britanniques,* the loo. *Veuillez agréer, monsieur, mes sentiments très distingués."*

Rogerson called to thank Felix.

"How's the weather?"

"Hot. Dry. I'm up to my neck in cactus."

"We're snowed in."

"I envy you."

"No, you don't."

"Let me know the outcome of the election."

"It should make *Mad* magazine."

"No wonder you're unhappy."

The Tuesday before Thanksgiving, Fort Elbow was hit by a storm that stopped traffic and got the vacation started a day earlier than scheduled. At the supermarket, Rogerson inspected the frozen turkeys but bought steak instead. He had never liked turkey. At the checkout counter he ran into Sylvia.

"Still here?"

"I canceled my trip. The storm."

"Where are you having Thanksgiving dinner?"

She fluttered her lashes. "With you, I hope."

"If you're free."

"I think I can fit you in."

The remark invited comment but at his age some modicum of dignity was required while at the checkout counter.

6

Thanksgiving dinner was steak and salad and sweet potatoes, eaten in the living room, watching a college game on television. At Rogerson's, at his insistence, which was perfectly okay with her. Sylvia was a little mellow after two martinis before and beer with the meal, and could have cared less about either of the teams playing.

"Wait until we field our own team."

"Rah rah."

"It doesn't matter who wins the election, Sylvia, we'll have a team."

"I can't tell whether you're happy or sad about it."

"I think Bellini will rue the day he succeeded at this. We'll be at the bottom of any league we're accepted by."

At least Matt watched sports without the sound. Football looked even sillier uncommented on, no roar of the crowd, no blare of the bands.

"That's the way life is to the deaf."

An odd thought. Imagine living in a silent world, seeing the gestures, the expressions, the moving mouths, hearing nothing. How ridiculous everything would seem. Or would it? Sylvia didn't feel like conceding the point to Rogerson.

"What about mime?"

"The Dolphins? Good team."

"The art form."

"Oh, I wouldn't go that far."

"Mime. Mimicry. Action without words." Sylvia stood and mimicked a mime for him. He loved it. He reached for her hand and pulled her down beside him on the couch.

"Let's live in sin together," he said huskily.

"It's okay with me."

"We can start with gluttony. Finish your steak."

During the afternoon his kids called. It seemed odd to think of him as a grandparent. His daughters were almost her age and the boy, well, the less said of him the better. A flight attendant. Because of the snow, it didn't get dark as early as usual and they let twilight take over the room without turning on the lights.

"No sound, no lights," he said.

"No action."

He kissed her, gently, no urgency, no passion either, just affection, undemanding, a grandfather's kiss.

"What comes after gluttony?"

He pinched her. "Weight Watchers."

Her slap landed gently on his beard.

He turned on a light beside the couch. "Want another beer?"

"Weight Watchers!"

He brought beer for the both of them, turned off the television, put on a Roger Miller CD and they talked about the election.

"Who do you think will win, Matt?"

"It's a toss-up. As in emetic."

"You're still for Laplace?"

"More than ever."

"I'm going to vote for Abe."

"I don't think of you as a senior faculty member."

"Do you know how long I've been here?"

"This is your tenth year."

"I'm surprised you know."

"Me too."

She did everything but ask him to let her stay, but his Catholic conscience was not dulled by drink. Maybe Thanksgiving had something to do with it. His kids calling. Remembering his wife. Marge. Such thoughts got Sylvia out of the mood, too. He walked her home, wanting a walk in the snow. Sylvia came outside again to watch him walk away, cap pulled down, head ducked, hands in his pockets kicking his way through the snow. She wished now she had asked him in and resorted to every wile she knew.

The weather continued bad, the Interstates were a mess, flights impossibly fouled up by cancellations and delays. Herman's self-serving prediction that the students would not be back and settled by election day turned out to be true. December 6 was overcast and cold with a bitter north wind. Voting booths had been set up in the Faculty Club, but when Sylvia got there at eleven there were only four attendants, two for Herman, two for Laplace.

"Voting slow?"

"What if they called an election and nobody came?"

An exaggeration, but the turnout was thin throughout the early afternoon. Rogerson came in and got on the phone and Old Bastards began to trickle in. Abe Herman and Laplace were keeping away from the polls, both having voted in the first half-hour. Sylvia, taking a cue from Matt, began to call people who hadn't voted.

"Does it really make any difference?" Grossteste asked.

"Not if you want Laplace to win."

"How can you tell who's ahead?"

"I'm guessing. But his people are working hard." She looked at Rogerson in the other phone booth.

In midafternoon, a van arrived filled with voters. Herb Laplace was at the wheel. Was this illegal? Only in the sense that he was driving without a licence. Rogerson said this with a smile but Sylvia took down the number and called the police.

"You say the man was driving the vehicle."

"He still is."

"But we don't know where, do we?"

"If you send someone to the Faculty Club on campus he will be coming back."

"I will give the information to the dispatcher."

"Thank you."

"Thank you for calling."

Why did she imagine the woman crumpling the note, if she had even made one, and arcing it into a wastebasket? Because it was a stupid call, that's why.

But twenty minutes later, Sylvia looked out and saw a squad car with swirling toplight parked in front of the van. Herb was at the wheel. Rogerson had gone out to see what was going on. Sylvia slipped into her coat and ran out.

The officer was looking at what Herb had just handed him.

"This seems to be in order. You shave off the beard, Mr. Rogerson?"

Herb nodded. "I couldn't stand the itching."

"He's not Rogerson," Sylvia cried. "That's not his licence."

Laplace was slipping the wallet into his pocket. The officer looked from Sylvia to Laplace.

"Can I see that again, sir?"

"Double jeopardy? No sirree."

"Let me see your licence, sir."

"I already showed you mine. Ask her for hers."

"She's not driving."

"Neither is my client," Rogerson said and hustled Laplace to the door of the club.

"Aren't you going to do something?" Sylvia asked the cop. He looked at Sylvia.

"Let me see your licence, ma'am."

"Oh, for heaven's sake."

Sylvia turned on her heel and marched back to the club. The squad car left with its siren screaming.

Handel was among the voters Laplace had just driven to the club. He was just emerging from the booth when Sylvia came back. Their eyes met and he looked away. He must have voted for Herb. Poor Abe. He had boasted of the way he had won Handel's vote.

When the polls closed at five, there were two hundred and three ballots to be counted, a miserable turnout, less than fifty percent of the electorate. Abe arrived for the counting, the bar was opened and diners began to drift in, among them several tenured faculty members who had forgotten this was the day they would elect the next chancellor. They did not seem completely downcast to have missed a chance to determine their own fate.

Sylvia and Rogerson were named official counters and performed the task at the same trestle table where voters had registered during the day. The crowd around the table grew as the counting progressed and the anxious faces of the candidates were conspicuous.

They made two piles of the counted ballots, each entering the vote on a tally and calling out the choice. With each mention of Herman, Abe's face shone, but it sank again when Laplace's name was called.

When the count was 87 Herman, 63 Laplace, Sylvia gave a grim smile to her candidate, but then the ballots cast after

Rogerson got on the phone began to register and the count tipped in Laplace's favor, 94 to 90. From that point on, there was an evenness in the count. Abe would inch ahead, Laplace would catch up and surpass him, then fall back as his opponent picked up ground.

And then, with one ballot remaining, the count stood at 101 to 101. Every eye was on the single uncounted ballot. Sylvia looked at Rogerson.

"You do it."

"No, you."

"Turn the damned thing over," Laplace demanded.

Sylvia did.

She read it out triumphantly.

Abe Herman had been elected the next chancellor of the Fort Elbow campus of the University of Ohio.

EPILOGUE

Twilight

When "Danny Boy" came on they stopped working and sang along, not so much carrying the tune as being carried along by the authoritative voice of John McCormack. There were tears in Herb's eyes.

"I love that song."

"You're a sentimentalist," Rogerson said.

"My mother was Irish."

"And hers before her."

They were clearing Herb's stuff out of the chancellor's office. A suite had been prepared for Laplace in the original building, a red brick structure with a dome on top. Herman, looking ahead, had decided that former chancellors should be treated with dignity and deference. Rose would continue with Herb as his secretary without any decrease of salary. Herb could only resent such generosity.

"Can you see Abe Herman behind that desk, Matt?"

"Not in this light."

"Everything's changing."

Herb stood in the middle of the room, a book dangling from each hand, shaking his head.

"Heraclitus."

"Who's he?"

"The new football coach."

"Ha."

During the past weeks Bellini had been floating rumors about the appointment of a football coach, and legendary coaches throughout the Midwest were forced to deny that they were contemplating the job. He overreached himself when he planted the story that Mike Ditka would be in town for talks with Chancellor Herman. The Bears' coach denied ever having heard of Fort Elbow, Ohio, but said his lawyers were trying to locate the school so they would know whom to sue.

"It's Bellini's way of keeping the pressure on Herman."

"Blitzing?"

Herb frowned.

"Rushing the quarterback."

"Yeah."

Rogerson removed the unread books from their shelves and put them in boxes. His attention was caught by a book that seemed to have been read. He turned to find Herb sitting at the desk, staring at the windows where fluffy flakes of snow floated in the winter air.

"Whose Spengler is this, Herb?"

"Mine. Pack it."

"You buy it secondhand?"

"You ought to read that book, Matt. He knew what he was talking about. The decline of the West."

"The twilight of the gods."

"Things go in cycles."

"And motorcycles."

But Herb was determined to be serious. "Danny Boy" had given way to the "Kerry Dances."

"Read the papers, watch television, look around you, Matt. Tell me the world isn't going to hell."

"We're old, Herb, that's all. It's not the world that's ending, it's us."

"Speak for yourself. I've got lots of miles in me yet."

"I'll drink to that."

"Would you like a drink?"

"There'll be plenty of that at the party."

The Faculty Club Christmas party would begin at five. It was now three-thirty. Herb crossed the room and opened the bar discreetly concealed behind a Madonna by Botticelli. He held a bottle of brandy to the light.

"I don't want to leave anything for Herman."

He poured two brandies and handed one to Rogerson. They clicked glasses. Rogerson toasted the cashiered chancellor.

"Welcome back to the ranks, Herb."

"Thanks a lot."

Herb's major fear, that he would have to return to the classroom to earn his salary, had been allayed by Herman's suggestion that Herb try to breathe some life into the Alumni Association.

"That's a relief," Rogerson said.

"Oh, I wouldn't have minded teaching."

"I was thinking of the students."

Herb finished his brandy and poured another. He held up the bottle, "Matt?"

Why not? The occasion was historic, in a minor way, a changing of the guard. Maybe not the end of civilization as we know it, but a kick in the slats to Herb.

"One vote, Matt. One lousy vote."

"I almost wished I'd voted for you."

Herb's eyes rounded in shock. The words of the "Kerry Dances" filled the room.

"You're kidding, aren't you?"

"Look at it this way, Herb. You might have won."

"That's what I'm saying."

"You were lucky you lost. Did you want to be carried out of here?"

The way Herb looked around the room it was clear he would have preferred dying in office. More likely he thought being chancellor was protection against mortality.

"Lillie coming to the party, Herb?"

"Was it you who told her about it?"

Meaning she was coming. She stopped by the office first, to take them to the club. The presence of Lillie aged Herb perceptibly. Grandma Laplace. She led them down to where she had defiantly left the car in the No Parking zone at the entrance of the building, motor running. Herb was aghast.

"Someone could just drive off in it."

"I locked the doors."

"With the key in the ignition?"

They faced one another and stared. Herb shook his head from side to side.

She said, "Don't you have your keys?"

"I don't drive anymore, remember?"

"Did you throw away your keys?"

"I'm not going to go all the way back to my office for them."

"They're in your office?"

Lillie shook her head. With the adroitness of the veteran wife, she had shifted the burden of guilt to her spouse's shoulders.

"Just leave it," Rogerson advised. "It won't go anywhere."

"With the motor running?" Lillie looked as if she were going to take a swing at him with her bag.

"They'll impound it," Herb groaned.

"You can pick it up at the police garage."

The wisdom of this prevailed and the three of them set off across the campus, the husband and wife moody and silent, Rogerson trying to get the tune of "Danny Boy" right. Herb stopped and looked back through the falling snow to the abandoned car.

"I only wish you hadn't left the lights on."

Fresh-fallen snow, lights shimmering through the leafless trees, the campus walks flanked by mounds of snow. They shuffled through the twilight to the Faculty Club. As they approached, cars were pulling into the lot in a steady stream, bundled-up figures heading for the doors from which, intermittently as they opened and closed, the sounds of Christmas escaped into the open air.

Inside, Herb waited for Lillie to emerge from the Ladies Room and Rogerson went on into the main meeting room, drawn by a glimpse of Sylvia. It took minutes to sidle through the crowd to where she was the cynosure of concupiscent glances. Her dress was silvery and daring; she seemed less to be wearing it than to have wrapped herself in it, casually, almost running out of material when she reached her bosom. Her golden hair was swept off her face and piled on top of her head. Her eyes shone with the realization that she was creating a sensation. Frege from Chemistry was talking to her.

"Lovely," Handel breathed at Rogerson's elbow.

The provost held a punch cup. Laura was nowhere in sight. Rogerson nodded at Sylvia. "Does the phrase 'custody of the eyes' mean anything to you?"

"A vicious divorce?"

Handel laid a hand on Rogerson's arm, to prevent further distractions. He intended to give a little lecture on monastic asceticism and he did. Rogerson lent him half an ear, disinclined at the moment to practice custody of the eyes himself. When he freed himself and joined Sylvia and Frege she turned bright, receptive gaze on Rogerson. He knew his admiration was written all over his bearded face.

"I've been looking for you," she said.

Abjectly and all too late, he remembered he had promised to bring her to the party. Imagine, making his entrance with Sylvia emerging like the fruits of the earth from the cornucopia of her gown.

"I was helping Herb."

"He's beyond it."

Frege leaned toward Rogerson, looking anxious. "Have you heard I'm being sued?"

"Tell me about it."

"Valerie's brother," Sylvia said. "Peter's parents are in it, too."

The university, more specifically the Chemistry Department, most specifically Frege, its chairman, were being sued for making arsenic available to a deranged young woman. It seemed a sign of the times. Responsibility shifted from agents to institutions, from deeds to circumstances.

"They'll win if it goes to court," Gil Mayhew said, when Rogerson and Sylvia came upon him in the crush at the bar. "Have you met Liz?"

The matron beside him smiled with lethal sweetness at Sylvia. Rogerson bowed. Liz Mayhew hadn't liked Marge either, and vice versa.

"If it goes to court?"

"We'll settle, of course."

They gave up on the bar. "You could die of thirst in here," Rogerson said.

"Wanna go?"

"Not until everyone has had a chance to see you."

Her laugh was girlish. Well, what woman does not want her beauty admired? For a moment, Rogerson entertained the wild theory that all women were beautiful, but Lillie Laplace grabbed his arm.

"Introduce me, Matt." Her tone was heavy with insinuation.

"This is Joy Roulette, Lillie. The new fencing coach. I thought you'd met. Joy, this is Mrs. Laplace."

"Fencing coach!" Lillie lowered her head and looked up at Rogerson.

Herb came into view. "Have you heard of Abe's baptism by fire?" he asked.

"Better watch your language."

"Relatives are suing the place for providing that girl with arsenic." Herb took this as a kind of vindication, God knows why. But triumph turned to raw envy as he took in Sylvia in her gown. "Hel-looo."

"Aren't you glad to be free again?" she asked him.

"Freedom can be abused, you know," Herb said, moving closer to her. But Lillie got a firm grip on his arm.

Carols gave way to dance tunes and Rogerson maneuvered Sylvia through the throng to the tune of "White Christmas."

"This is like dancing with a Christmas present."

She drew back and gave him a lidded look.

But repartee was wasted in the crush on the dance floor. He drew her closer and they moved as much as those around them permitted. Rogerson would not have wanted to see this scene with the sound off.

The next time they tried the bar they succeeded. Bourbon and Scotch. Stick to the basics.

"Which is mine?" Sylvia asked.

"Either or."

Sylvia chose Scotch.

"Here's to the girl who lives on the hill."

Not six feet away, Abe Herman, in a dark suit and a festive red vest, was holding court. The first corrupting taste of power. Had anyone paid any attention to him at last year's party?

Turning away, Rogerson caught a glimpse of Carlotta, gliding through the happy throng like Natasha toward some Prince Andrei of her dreams. Sylvia liked the allusion.

"She's so good on *War and Peace*."

"What else is there?"

By the time dinner was served, taste buds had been dulled by strong drink, and the food was widely praised and little consumed. Wine flowed. With dessert, they received a few words from the new chancellor. Abe had trouble with the PA system and his words seemed to be coming in from outer space, but his best wishes for the various seasons observed by members of the university community were audible. He received a standing ovation.

Sylvia looked at Rogerson. He nodded and pushed away from the table.

Her car was in the lot and he sat in the passenger seat feeling like a gigolo and saying so.

"Don't get your hopes up."

The radio had gone on with the engine and they were surrounded by seasonal music as they followed her low beams into the still-swirling snow. Reality seemed to have lost its edge. Aside from an arthritic twinge in his knee, Rogerson felt tip-top. She pulled up in front of his house and did not turn off the motor.

"Come in."

"Sure?"

He reached over and twisted the key.

* * *

"Where is it you're going for the holidays?"

"San Miguel de Allende."

"Where's that?"

"Mexico. Have you ever been there?"

They were sitting in the living room, Rogerson in a chair, Sylvia distributed on the couch, as comfortable as she could be in her elegant gown.

"Is it warm?"

"Matt, you'd love it. Come along."

He imagined himself under a semitropical sun, drinking the local wine, enjoying a pagan interlude. Nothing in Sylvia's moral code stood in the way of a little romp down Mexico way. She was a child of her time, sex only contingently related to reproduction and thus permanence. They were worlds apart. Why did they get along so well?

"Wouldn't it be fun?" She had put her feet on the floor and was leaning toward him.

"What a blouseful of goodies."

She ignored that but she was not displeased. "We can call the airline in the morning. Even if we don't have the same flight . . ."

She was caught up in the idea now. He listened to her enthused description of the town, the dusty streets, half-starved dogs dragging themselves from one patch of shade to another, the cantinas. She knew places Americans did not frequent. He could see the sun on the adobe walls, the tile roofs, the balcony from which they would look out over the valley. The better it sounded the surer he was he would not go.

Thoughts of Amanda disturbed the inviting idyll Sylvia described. Rogerson felt he had been irresponsible with that troubled girl. Just because Psychological Services was fraudulent did not mean mental illness did not exist. Was Amanda mad? He had been flattered by her attention, had given her bits of his standard repertoire, canned wisdom for the masses, bits and pieces of lectures he had given over the years, available on demand to dazzle the young. He should have known she was crazy when she nominated him for chancellor.

Sylvia came and sat on the arm of his chair. Looking up at her, he could see she was waiting for a reply.

"I don't have a visa."

"You don't need a visa."

"MasterCard okay?"

"Matt, be serious."

He moved over and tugged her down beside him.

"You overestimate me."

"How will we ever know?"

"Take my word."

He would let her think him impotent to avoid hurting her feelings. An odd standoff, that, his soul and her feelings.

"Well, it was a pretty thought," she sighed.

He would have appreciated a little more persistence on her part. "Maybe next year."

"You'll be cured then?"

When she left, he stood in the doorway and watched her walk out to her car. She brushed accumulated snow from the rear window and let the wipers clear the windshield. The sound of the motor, then the cone of her lights alive with snow. She gave a little toot of her horn before pulling away.

He turned off the porch light, carried glasses and bottles to the kitchen, put out the lamps. The house was not completely dark even with all the lights out. As he often did now, Rogerson walked through the rooms of the house in which he had raised his family, where he had lived with his discontented wife. The place was haunted with his memories.

He had not yet gone upstairs when the phone rang.

"Matt?" It was Sylvia.

"Get home all right?"

"Think about Mexico, Matt. We'll talk again in the morning."

Standing in his darkened house, Rogerson smiled. "I'll think about it."

"Think seriously. All this snow, Matt. You really should get away."

He hung up and went slowly upstairs. Winter was his season and snow his element. Rogerson did not find this a difficult truth to accept.

RALPH MCINERNY, author of the Father Dowling mysteries and other novels, including *Connolly's Life, The Noonday Devil,* and *Leave of Absence,* is the Michael P. Grace Professor of Medieval Studies at the University of Notre Dame. *The Search Committee* completes the Rogerson trilogy that began with *Jolly Rogerson* and continued with *Rogerson at Bay*.